Falling for the Voice

Falling for the Voice

MAG MAURY

WARM PUBLISHING

Translated from the French by Rafaela Reece

WARM PUBLISHING
El Paso, Texas
www.warmpublishing.com

Original title: *Fast Games*
published by Éditions Addictives
Paris, France

ISBN: 978-1-7345961-5-1

Table of Contents

1. The Curse of the Pigeon

"No, no, no, nooooooo!"

Not today! Why did my bed have to take me hostage today?

Is it conspiring with my alarm clock or what? Why didn't it ring? The day of my job interview…

I leap to my feet and wail in frustration, "Whyyy???"

Come on, get going, action-reaction, I only have an hour to get ready and get to my interview! I hate it when things don't go according to plan! What a disaster!

Action stations! I go into warrior mode and get showered and dressed as fast as possible: I pull on some jeans, a blouse, and my boots (luckily, I prepared my outfit carefully last night), then add a little makeup. If I'm lucky, I'll get there! I give myself a quick once-over in the mirror: hmm, yes, that should do! A spray of perfume, and I'll be—"Shit, it burns! It burns! Arrrgh! My eye!"

Great start! That's just what I need: a red eye at a first interview! Honestly… Grrrrr!!!

Come on, stay calm! Try to look on the bright side. Umm… At least my retina smells good!

I'm 28, and today I'm interviewing for a temporary waitressing job at the Green Country pub, which might lead to permanent work. I can't afford to blow this interview. Not with my apartment to pay for! I can't let Chloé, my best friend who lives with me, pay the rent alone while I'm trying to find work!

Sure, our little nest is no palace, but we like it. It's spacious with a small open-air courtyard, it's bright, and big enough to give us both the independence we need. We've known each other for ten years. It's been a long and wonderful friendship, and now we've been living together for two years.

Chloé is the impulsive one: she's as spontaneous as I am cautious. She's a year older than I am and is head sales representative for a cosmetics chain. We were lucky to find each other! We couldn't be more different, but somehow, we make a great pair. If I didn't have her, I'd stay shut up at home like a hermit in his cave! She's a real party animal and is responsible for my finest hangovers...

Actually, while we're on the subject, I have Chloé to thank for the brilliant idea she had last night... surprise drinks, in the hope that white wine would relax me for my interview today. Thanks to her, the *Fraggle Rock* puppets are holding an after party in my head!

I pull the door shut behind me and run down the stairs two at a time: I still have twenty minutes to get to the pub!

As I sprint down the street, I savor the feeling of the warm spring air rushing past me. There's no denying it: living somewhere as sunny as the south of France sure has its advantages! Lost in thought and stressed about what lies ahead, my heart just about stops when an unidentified projectile suddenly hits me smack on the cheek. In an instant, I'm in ninja mode, ready to take on my assailant!

It's a goddamn pigeon?!

A stupid... goddamn... pigeon just flew into my face!

Seriously? A street full of people and I'm the one to get hit by a pigeon?!

Suddenly, I feel alone in the world. My eye is still streaming, my brain is drenched in Dordogne's finest wine, and now I get attacked by a pigeon! But it's all good, just so long as my cheek doesn't start to swell up. I get the feeling this is going to be a very, very, very long day...

A few moments later, I'm standing outside the pub.

The black and gold sign stretches across the front, with the names of the bands that are playing there just below. Suddenly, the fame of the venue knocks all the confidence out of me. Surely I'm not going to chicken out now? When I replied to the ad, I didn't think about the reputation of the place. The answer came quickly, and I didn't have much time to think it over. But now, as I stare at the super-trendy-looking building, I'm starting to feel a little less brave. Still, there's no use in turning back now!

I take my courage in both hands, push open the heavy door with its carved handles, and step into the huge room, with a counter running all the way around it. Holy shit! How many people work behind this bar?

After the bright light outside, it takes my eyes a few seconds to adjust to the dusky atmosphere. When they do, I can make out the people sitting at a table in a corner. The decor is fascinating! Lots of booths with black benches, gold-edged tables separated by smoked glass, creating a warm, modern, and resolutely country atmosphere.

There are more tables in the main area, and a huge stage at the back, overlooking a dance floor, which I have to admit could rival any nightclub in the region.

The exposed beams and wood floor give this place its own look, which really appeals to me. Suddenly, one of the men gets up and walks over to me. He's bald, with a goatee, and has a commanding presence. When he speaks, his voice is deep and smooth, "Hello, can I help you?"

I mustn't lose it, not now. For a moment, I wonder if he will notice that I can only see out of one eye and that my cheek is all swollen.

I cannot let him see that I'm stressed, that's all that matters. "Hi, I'm Charlotte Moreau. I have a meeting about the waitressing job you advertised."

He holds a hand out to me, with an expression that I can't quite read, and asks me to follow him into his office.

He's an impressive man, with a certain air of confidence. I take a deep breath and follow him. Fingers crossed!

An hour later I come out of the pub, my smile almost splitting my face in two! *Yes, yes, yes!* I got the job! I'm elated! I can't believe my luck. It turns out the boss, Terrence, is a really friendly guy, and he made me feel at ease right way. I start work in two days, and he said I should come back tomorrow evening at 9 PM, to get a feel for the place, the bar and how things work there.

My first reflex is to call Chloé and share my news with her. As expected, I have to hold my cell phone away from my ear, to save my eardrums from her high-pitched squeals! She has the annoying habit of turning up the volume when she gets carried away. I'm excited, but a little nervous. I had to give up my art studies very early to earn a living. Jobs in the region are hard to find, and this one is a real godsend. I know how to wait tables, and I'm used to dealing with crowds. But after my little misadventure, I lost my last job. Now, after two years off work recovering, I'm glad to have the opportunity to work again.

◎ ◎ ◎

The next evening, at exactly 9 PM, I arrive at the door of the Green Country pub. People are already pushing to get in, and as I slip through, I notice there's a crowd inside too. The whole place is buzzing, and the music is in full swing. When I think that the night is only just getting started, I can't help but wonder what it will be like in a couple of hours. Terrence welcomes me with his widest smile. We keep things informal, which I like: it feels friendlier. None of my previous bosses were so welcoming. They were all pretty stuffy and distant. Terrence starts by showing me around. He introduces me to Chris and Tommy at the bar, then Sam and Lucas who do table service. All four of them look at me like I've washed up here by mistake. Can anyone tell me where the girls are? I'm outnumbered here.

I ask Terrence when the girls start work, so I can meet them. He bursts out laughing, winks and answers, "You'll see so many females tomorrow, you'll be glad you're the only one working here!"

Pretty puzzling, as far as answers go...

I guess my concern must show on my face, because Terrence looks at me and softens his voice, "Don't worry, Charlie, you'll do just fine!"

As we continue our tour, he explains that on Fridays and Saturdays at 10 PM there are live bands, and the atmosphere is pretty animated.

Okay, now that I can deal with! I've worked at the Comédie

Opera house in Montpellier in the summer season, and I've managed a hotel, so I'm sure I can cope with a bit of a crowd. It's going to be okay, or at least that's what I try to tell myself!

Guitar and bass arrangements start to fill the room. I turn around and see several people dashing around, doing sound checks.

The boss tells me to go and get to know the team, and says he'll see me tomorrow night at nine.

I sit at the bar and introduce myself to Chris and Tommy, who are twins. They are tall with brown hair, and they work in perfect tandem. There's nothing they can't do with a cocktail shaker! They greet my shyness with big, kind smiles, and they offer to help me if need be.

"Seriously, don't hesitate to ask if you feel a bit lost," Chris says.

"Absolutely, we'd be more than happy to help," adds Tommy, skillfully mixing a cocktail.

I appreciate their spontaneous generosity, and thank them for being so helpful. It makes it easier for me to relax.

We chat for a while, then Sam and Lucas come and join us.

All four of them gently tease me.

"Ha-ha, to tell the truth, we thought Charlie was a guy!"

I plant my hands on my hips and raise an eyebrow. "Not a problem, is it?"

Sam is quick to answer, holding up both hands in surrender. "Oh, no! No worries, especially with everything we need to do this weekend. We'll be glad to have an extra pair of hands. Anyway… I'd rather have a girl like you to look at than…"

Lucas smacks him on the back of the head to shut him up, glares at him, then turns to me, looking embarrassed. "What Sam means is that having a female presence on the team is nicer than having yet another guy!"

Suddenly, I find myself wondering what the recruitment process was like for them! Why are there only men here, and why are they all so sexy? The whole thing is a bit of a mystery.

Without exception, they are all proudly exhibiting tattoos and piercings.

Sam and Lucas ask me if I feel ready for tomorrow, as they

try to reassure me. They'll do all they can to help. The relaxed atmosphere of camaraderie makes me feel more confident about my new job.

I say goodbye to the guys, walk past the bar, and as I am leaving, the four of them chant in chorus: "Goodbye, Charlie!"

I turn to them, laughing at the allusion to the movie, *Charlie's Angels*, and walk right into a closet. No, it's not a closet. It's a man. A very tall man. Damn, he's muscly! Sam, Chris, Tommy and Lucas burst out laughing. That pack of jackals, they did it on purpose!

I move back, my foot catches on the step behind me, and I feel myself falling backwards, but the stranger grabs me firmly and holds me up. I pull myself free, mumbling "thanks" and look at him properly. With his cap on backwards covering his hair, his steely blue eyes focused on me, and not a trace of a smile, he introduces himself in a suave voice. "Luke Matthews."

Wow! Quite the conversationalist. It seems a full sentence is too much to ask of Skywalker here!

I answer him just as coolly, only giving him my first name. Then I turn around and make my escape.

◎ ◎ ◎

Back at the apartment, I don't know what to think. Chloé, overflowing with energy like an overcharged battery, bombards me with questions, some of which are pretty twisted.

"Maybe we'll get lucky and you'll learn to let go a bit!" she adds eagerly.

She's convinced my life is more *Seven Years in Tibet* than *Dirty Dancing*. I have to admit she's kind of right... A nice hot shower, that's what I need to get over my evening! I can't help thinking about that Luke guy. Not very friendly at first sight. But he's built like a Greek God! I don't know him, but I don't think he could have been any colder to me if I'd been a psychopath!

Sure, he might have gotten into my head, but...

Just remember, a handsome face can hide a total creep!

I get out of the shower, wrap my robe around me, and lie on the bed. Chloé comes in five minutes later, puts some music on, sits cross-legged on my bed, and smiles at me. The sound of jazz starts to fill my room. She has learned that music is the best therapy for me. She knows me inside and out. She's been there for me for years now, and we've overcome life's challenges together, like sisters. Thanks to her, my eyes are soon drifting shut, and I let myself sink into a healing sleep.

2. Mojitos and Missiles

When I open my eyes, it's 8 AM. The smell of coffee coaxes me out of bed, and I am soon sitting at the kitchen table with Chloé. She pours me a big mug of coffee.

"Today: shopping, sweetie," she says. "You start your job tonight, so you might as well arrive in fine form. And maybe you'll meet the man of your dreams there. Who knows? Come on, let's get going!"

I can't help but admire her. She's always so positive and full of energy, like she's powered by some alien energy source. "OK, OK, I'm up for the shopping spree, but just remember, we're not living a fairytale. In this life, if you lose a shoe after midnight, it just means you're drunk!"

"Drunk or not, if it can bring some balance into your life, I don't see any harm in it!"

I turn to her and tell her calmly, "One: being drunk at work is a novel idea, but coming from you, nothing surprises me! Two: when I'm drunk, I can tell you my balance is far from optimum! Three: I'm happy just the way I am!"

Having said my piece, I go and get ready to shop. I have to admit, I like her plan.

We go out to face the Saturday crowds and spend over four hours emptying our bank accounts and filling our wardrobes. We sit down for a snack on the terrace of a restaurant and then go say hi to her sister, Emily, at her tattoo studio.

The two of them couldn't be more different. Emily is pretty alternative: shaved head, tattoos, and a ridiculous number of piercings, and yet she is so sweet, a really wonderful friend.

"Hi, girls! So, Charlie, how was your induction at the Green Country pub? Go on, spill!"

"Oh! Well, let's just say you wouldn't be out of place there. It looks like they're all competing to see who has the biggest tattoo or the most piercings."

"Seriously? And the women?"

"What women?! Let's just say I'm the only female on the team for the moment."

"So, Sis, fancy going out tonight?" Chloé says with a delighted grin.

"I wouldn't say no! I've been working my butt off these days."

We chat over coffee, and my anxiety melts away, like it always does when we get together. After all the laughs and pastries, I feel ready to face the evening. The afternoon flies by, and we finally decide to go home.

I take a quick shower, then put on some worn jeans, my boots, and a slate-gray shirt. Simple and practical. I let my long, blonde hair down and put on some light makeup. Chloé approves of my choice, even if she would have liked for me to wear something sexier. She's always telling me to stop hiding myself under safe, traditional clothes, but I can't see myself ever doing it. Finally ready, I head out the door as she showers me with kisses and hugs of encouragement.

When I push the pub door open, I freeze at the sight of all the people inside. I wasn't expecting such an impenetrable crowd!

I join Chris and Tommy behind the bar, and they give me a warm hug. I put down my bag and ask them where they need me most. Since Terrence isn't there, they tell me I'll be starting my evening waiting tables.

Sam and Lucas appear behind me, give me a squeeze hello and show me the area I'll be in charge of: around fifteen tables near the stage. Time to start! I pick up my handset and begin taking orders immediately. Everyone is shuffling around and jostling each other, waiting impatiently for the concert to begin. The orders start pouring in. At the bar, I notice that the twins are in full swing. Their shakers are performing a frenzied waltz, and pints of beer are sliding along the counter with precision.

The audience suddenly surges towards the stage, and I realize that the band is setting up. The first chords ring out, to screams from the dense crowd. Well, when I say "crowd," what I actually mean is a swarm of women, trying to elbow their way to the front. It looks like the beginning of Black Friday!

The women in the middle of the herd are packed in so tight they can't budge a limb. When the first song, "Kill the Light," starts, I have to admit that the singer's enchanting voice is, well… fiery!

The acoustic guitar combined with the unique sound of his singing leaves me speechless! When I look up, I can't believe my eyes. Luke Matthews! Holy shit! I struggle to concentrate. I mustn't let myself get distracted. Yes, I need to focus on my orders; that's what I have to do! When my eyes meet his, I almost trip. I just dodged a bullet. Twice in two days; I'm on a roll!

What is that gleam in his eyes? Satisfaction? Is he mocking me? Then, he gives me a smile that could make the panties of any woman in that crowd melt away, while this chick gives me a look that could kill.

I go back to the bar to pick up my tray loaded with beers, and Chris comes over to me: "Everything okay, Charlie? You're doing great, Simon and Lucas are really proud of you! And not many people get their seal of approval when it comes to table service!"

Touched by his kind words, I go back to my tables with a boosted ego. But not without checking Luke out in passing. Shit! The way he moves his hips, he's driving everyone wild! You really would have to have a blind eye to work here without getting distracted.

I need another hit from that pigeon!

As I serve the table their drinks, the chick who was shooting daggers at me a few minutes ago pushes me hard. I stumble into a table, breaking a beer tankard as I fall. My head hits the broken glass, and I cut my lip. She screams at me that I'm hassling her when I'm supposed to be there to serve her. Shocked, I lurch backwards. "What the hell is wrong with you? Are you completely insane?!"

She lifts her hand, about to strike. I protect my face with my forearm, but Skywalker leaps off the stage, grabs her firmly by the wrist, and holds her back, giving her a deadly look. "Don't even think about it!"

Then he calls out to Sam. "Put this outside for me!" he says in an icy voice.

The enraged woman starts screaming and cursing in her native language, trying to wrestle free from Sam's grip, but eventually, despite all her struggling, she finds herself out in the street.

I hear a break being announced over the speakers, and before I know it, Luke is pulling me towards the kitchen. I'm in shock from the scuffle, and I feel completely drained. Great, I'm sure to get chewed out and lose my job when Terrence finds out about this.

But how could I have known what would happen? Bitter tears sting my eyes, and it takes all the strength I have to hold them back.

I'm preparing myself for the wrath of my savior when he gently places his hands on my waist, picks me up and puts me down on the edge of the sink. He uses his index finger to gently lift my chin, so that our eyes meet. "Are you okay? That's a nasty cut, let me clean it for you."

I watch him getting out gauze and some antiseptic. My brain desperately tries to find a logical link between the unpleasant man I met yesterday and the attentive, concerned man standing in front of me now. Very gently, he disinfects my swollen lip, his eyes never leaving mine. In fact, I think this is the precise moment that my brain (like a coward!) decides to abandon me and go on a road trip by itself. I try to regain some composure. "Sorry about all this, but I didn't provoke her. I've just started here—I understand you'll have to report it to Terrence. I guess I'll lose my job. What rotten luck!"

He raises an astonished eyebrow and stares at me for a long time.

"What on earth are you talking about? Be quiet and let me sort this out. You get attacked doing your job, and you think you're going to get fired? Are you sure you didn't knock your head? Hard?"

"I'm totally fine. I'm just saying that getting into a fight on my first day isn't the best way to prove myself!"

"Don't forget where you are, there are plenty of fights here. I'd advise you not to cross that woman again: she's a total nutjob!"

"What? You know that fruitcake? Wait, let me guess... She's your ex?"

"Uh, umm... Well, it was a mistake, really," he answers dryly.

"A... a mistake! I don't call that a mistake. I call that an epic fail! In the future, choose your mistakes more carefully. They hurt, dammit!"

He gives me an amused smile. "I've finished, do you feel well enough to get back to work?" he says.

"Yes, I think so. Thanks, Luke."

"It's Matthews, or Matt. Nobody calls me Luke."

"Oh! Okay then: thanks, Matthews."

"Right, you stick to the bar with Chris and Tommy for the rest of the evening."

"What? No, honestly, I can..."

"Go behind the bar, it's safer!"

"And shall I curtsy before I go, boss?"

He gives me a dazzling smile, and just for a second, I think I glimpse a speck of defiance in it.

He picks me up by the waist as if I were a feather, and puts me down on the floor, but his powerful hands stay on my hips. Wow, he really is tall. I'm only 5'2. He makes me feel like a doll. His musky, woody scent wafts up my nostrils...

What am I doing, glued to the floor like this?

Come on, move, do something, at least try to string two words together, you nitwit!

I curse myself for being so bewildered by his closeness.

"Are you okay? Not dizzy?" Matthews asks.

"Yes, I'm fine."

I step away from him, a little too quickly perhaps, trying to get my hormones to stop bouncing around. By the look of the enormous grin on his face, he's noticed how flustered I am...

Dammit!

We return to the main room, and I join the twins behind the bar. Both of them run over to me. They reassure me and stay by my side, chatting and making me laugh, so that I feel the built-up tension beginning to subside.

Matt goes back to his place on stage, and in the blink of an eye, the atmosphere brightens. Wow, he's talented! Really talented! Song after song, each as amazing as the last. The orders are coming in thick and fast at the bar. The pace is intense but I'm enjoying it.

Suddenly, through the crowd, Chloé and Emily catch my eye. When did they get here? They walk over to me, grinning from ear to ear. "Don't think we didn't notice how you deceived us! When did you mention that you were working with team sexy?" Chloé fires at me point-blank.

"Okay, okay! It's been a rough night, don't make it any worse! How long have you been here?"

"We just arrived, actually, just as you were coming out of the closet with Mr. Dynamite," she answers, pointing towards the stage at Matthews, who is busy doing something very provocative with his hips…

This guy will be the end of me.

"Next time, make sure he eats first!" Emily says, noticing my cut lip, teasing me openly.

Ha ha ha, very funny!!!

Emily turns my head with her hand so she can look at my cut.

"What happened, anyway?"

"Oh! Well, let's just say that one of His Majesty's groupies took her wrath out on me…"

"Wow, not a great start, then!"

Chloé takes me by the shoulders and looks worried for a moment. I turn and point at my lip. "Is it gross?"

She smiles, offering silent reassurance.

"You're a bit beaten up, but it should heal quickly," Emily answers, as tactful as ever.

"Thanks, girls, I see I can count on your support! I'm on the brink of hell, and you're ready to push me over. Nice!"

Suddenly, we're laughing uncontrollably, and I look at my friends warmly. I love them! "I hate you both!"

"We love you too! Come on, what are we drinking?"

"MOJITOS of course," Chloé answers.

I keep serving customers and chatting, while the girls drown a stressful week in cocktails. I busy myself keeping everything tidy behind the bar, and get the orders out with ease.

I see the guys getting curious about my friends. They even try to approach them, which makes me smile.

It's getting late: almost 2 AM. The pub starts emptying out, and the music volume drops. I am busy cleaning a few glasses that are sitting in the tub, when suddenly, there are two hands on either side of the sink… two arms on either side of me. No point turning around: I know it's him, Matt. His enchanting scent is so… so him. He leans towards me, moves his lips close to my neck and murmurs in my ear, "Everything okay?"

I almost faint. What is this jerk playing at? Is he trying to torture me or what? Stop! I have to get out of here! "Yes, thanks, I'm finishing my shift soon, then I can go home!"

I escape his arms and try to hide my disarray. He leans on the end of the bar, his arms folded, and looks me up and down unashamedly. This guy really has it all: life is so unfair! His red T-shirt clings to his muscular body, revealing powerful, tattooed arms. His jeans hug his thighs perfectly and leather bracelets decorate his wrists.

Whoa, talk about pleasure in a package! I really have to get a grip. It's official, common sense has deserted me!

MISSING:

Brain, barely used,
Currently in training,
Can be rebellious, disappeared suddenly today…
Please contact Charlie!

It really is time I went home! I glance at Chloé, who seems to have her eyes glued to Sam… There's no stopping that woman! Unfortunately, this is when Lucas and Tommy decide to propose a toast to my first night. Shit, I'm in no mood for this! Matt seems to find my failed escape attempt amusing. He gives me a charming smile and pushes me towards the rest of the team at the end of the bar. Sam and Chris are also up for giving my arrival the celebration it deserves, serving drinks after closing the pub. The girls, who were waiting to leave with me, join us, and we launch into an animated conversation about tattoos.

"So, Emily, you have a tattoo parlor in town?" Lucas asks.

"Yes, I've had it for a few years now. I see you've got a work in progress yourself."

As I listen to my friends talking to the boys, I realize that Matthews has come over. He is standing just behind me. Unsettled at the thought of him being so close, I don't quite know how to act. I feel like I'm being scrutinized, and the sensation it gives me is strange. I guess he must have noticed my discomfort, because he moves even closer and whispers in my ear: "What about you, kitten, have you got any hidden tattoos? What treasures are you hiding?"

The mojitos have really gone to my head, and suddenly, I feel myself flush with heat. But are the cocktails really to blame? "Don't call me that!"

Without even answering Matthews's question, I look at my watch and decide it really is time to go home. It's already 3 in the morning.

Luckily for me, the pub is closed tomorrow. We are just getting ready to leave when Sam offers to give us a ride. So we leave the pub and head for Sam's SUV.

Ten minutes later, back at our apartment, I can't wait to take refuge in my bed. I leave Chloé chatting with Sam and hurry inside. Goddammit, I'm a mess!

PERSONAL CHECK-UP:

Energy: low battery
Stomach: ugh
Brain: Reported missing
Balance: shaky
Feelings: total tornado
Verdict: bed... now!

Miserably, I make my way to my bedroom, slip on an extra-large T-shirt and collapse into bed.

Yes, but... a couple of voices in my head want to sleep, and another one wants to know if penguins have knees!

Nevertheless, I eventually sink into a deep sleep, where strange creatures are twerking to country music.

A promising start!

3. Intrusion and Hairballs

I'm under a blue hippopotamus who is dancing to "Pump it Up" and repeating my name over and over again.

"Charlie… Psssst! Charlie… Wake up, Charlie!"

Lost in a fog, I make a heroic attempt to work my way out of it. Logically speaking, if I can manage to open one eye, the second should follow… Well, I did say, "logically." Oh hell! Connecting my neurons is a delicate operation right now. I can make out Chloé, kneeling at the foot of my bed, using all of the diplomatic skills at her disposal to find out whether or not I'm in working order.

"You okay?"

Well, to be honest, no! I'm not okay… not at all! Nevertheless, I manage to get three words out: "Let me diiiieee…!"

I pull the covers over my head, trying to escape my roommate's probing gaze. Having one last drink when you're already well and truly hammered is as stupid as putting biscotti in a toaster! I try to move, but my body won't cooperate. Hello muscle aches… and hello headache! Chloé is looking at me sympathetically, while desperately trying to hold back the howls of laughter that are bursting to get out. She sits down on the edge of my bed.

"Do you want the good news or the bad news first?" she hesitantly asks.

I get the sinking feeling she's going to wreck my day before it's even begun. "Go wild: the bad news!"

"We're out of coffee!"

Noooo! Not that! Anything but that!

I want to bash my head against the wall in frustration, but it feels like I already have. No coffee! My only source of comfort, the only thing that could possibly make me feel better after a drinking spree, the thing about which I have been unfailingly passionate since I was sixteen. "And the good news?"

Suddenly, a funny look comes over her face. She sits back a little and hesitates before answering. "Uh, well, umm… Matt is… well… He's in the kitchen and… he's waiting for you…"

I suddenly feel very alone…

That's good news?!

Option one: Go back to dancing in the fog with my blue hippopotamus!

Option two: Strangle Chloé to death with her own hair for playing such a dirty trick on me!

Option three: Hide in the back of my closet, pretending I have an emergency to deal with in Narnia!

I take a long, deep breath before giving her a second chance to say something that makes sense. "Would you please tell me what you're rambling about!" I say, trying to keep the irritation out of my voice.

I watch her writhe, staring her down. I know that after hearing my tone, she is considering every one of my growled words very carefully indeed.

"I plead innocent, he really gave me no choice. When I heard knocking at the door, I didn't expect to see him in the hallway, as you can imagine. But he insists he has to see you and talk to you. I tried to tell him that, knowing you, it was a terrible idea, but he's stubborn! Really stubborn! I don't know what you did to him in the closet last night, but he seems determined to get a second helping! You've got to admit it though, he's seriously sexy…"

"Nooo! I don't want to see him. I have nothing to say to him. I've already thanked him and… and… well, that's it! Done! I'm a mess here. I'm not even sure I can get out of bed…"

With an evil little smile, she quips back, "Oh right. You already thanked him, did you? Would you like to tell me exactly what you did to thank him? Sooner or later, I'll get it out of you, you know that! Still, I have to admit you look rough, Charlie. I don't think he'll agree to leave, though. He seems pretty determined."

I narrow my eyes at her dirty mind. The memories of my run-in with that skank slip back into my head, and the pain from my swollen lip only serves to induce panic. "That bad? What do you mean, I look rough?"

"Are we talking about your hair, or the state of your lip?" she asks, unable to control her laughter any longer as she points to my reflection in the mirror.

The state of affairs is worse than I imagined. Now that's what I call a shock of hair... with a capital S for shock. Is that even my hair? It looks like porcupines have taken up residence on my head. And as for my lip... Its only advantage is that it might detract attention from my hair. The split seems to be turning a deep purple, and my normally rather thin bottom lip has swollen to huge proportions.

Better than Picasso!

"Okay, let's call a cease-fire on the jokes, Charlie. How do you feel? Does it hurt? Do you need anything?"

"Yes, you know what? I need you to go back into the kitchen, tell him I'm dead and you'll call him about the funeral. I can't even face my own reflection, let alone him!"

As Chloé gets up to leave the room, she can't help giving me a reassuring smile. "One day, you're going to have to let the world in again."

I know she's right. I know she worries about me, and I also know that without her by my side, I would probably have given up. Her unfailing friendship and her presence in my life have allowed me to move forward, knowing I have someone to support me.

When she opens my bedroom door, Matt is there, leaning against the wall with his arms folded. He is wearing a black shirt with the sleeves rolled up and the bottom of his biceps just peeping out, unbearably well-fitting, worn jeans, and his black boots. I've never seen a man look so good in jeans. It's like they've been painted onto his muscular thighs. Oh my God! He just oozes sex appeal.

He leans towards Chloé, mumbles something in her ear (unfortunately, I can't hear what), lets her leave and comes into my bedroom, taking care to close the door behind him.

Are you kidding me? What does he think he's doing?

"STOP!!! Don't come one step closer! Chloé, get back in here or I'll lynch you! What the hell are the two of you playing at? What is this half-baked plan? Get OUT! I would like to remind you that this is my refuge, my bedroom, my personal space, not Grand Central Station, for crying out loud! Does nobody here give a damn about my privacy?"

Clearly not the slightest bit concerned by my outburst, he just looks at me and smiles. "Hey, shh, kitten. Calm down. Put those claws away. I'm not going to attack you or leap on you, and I'm certainly not going to do anything inappropriate! You don't kick someone while they're down!"

"You don't... What? I'll kick *you*, I'm telling you! I'm not your kitten, or anything of yours! You just show up here, say those tasteless things, and I'm supposed to... calm down?"

I start cursing again, grabbing my pillow to throw it at him. Unfortunately, he dodges it easily, starts laughing again, and comes a step closer. "I just want to talk to you. Are you going to calm down? Or are you going to start coughing up hairballs?"

I arm myself with a second pillow, ready to attack again, but the sudden pain in my side makes me wince, which, of course, Matt notices. Suddenly, his gaze darkens, and the concern in his eyes sends a jolt through me.

I let the pillow drop down beside me, suddenly dizzy. In one stride, he's kneeling at my bedside, looking at me long and hard. I'm weary all of a sudden, so tired... My head feels like it's about to burst, and my ribs are throbbing with pain.

"May I?" he asks quietly, gesturing that he wants to sit beside me.

I nod silently, shuffling to the left to make room for him. Cursing my anger, I stare hard at my comforter so that I don't have to meet his eyes. Why does this guy have such an effect on me? I hate myself for feeling so vulnerable right now, but his scent fills my room, and having him so close to me throws me for a loop.

Magnetic... Yes, that's the word! This guy is magnetic.

Come on, let's be honest, finding yourself in your bedroom, hung over from the night before, in a rather shaky physical state, wearing an extra-large Mickey Mouse T-shirt and white shorties, in front of a man you hardly know with a physique even a nun couldn't resist... it would make anyone flustered!

"I came to see how you are, Charlie. Terrence was worried too," he says softly, sitting down beside me.

"I'm fine. At least, I think I am. Nothing too serious: just a cut lip. No reason to barge in here uninvited. Now will please you go home, let Terrence know I'm okay, and leave me to agonize in peace? I'll recover!"

He slowly slides his index finger under my chin and lifts my head so that I'm forced to look him in the eye.

Bad idea...

His gaze is so deep and perplexing, it blows my mind. This blockhead is going to leave me gaping like a fish out of water if he keeps staring at me like this.

Houston! We have a problem! Cannot retrieve data! Crash imminent...

His thumb lightly brushes my lower lip, moving back and forth. The gesture is much too intimate. He keeps talking, ignoring my protests. "Given the state you're in, I think it seems perfectly justified. What happened last night never should have happened. I'm sorry you fell victim to that girl. I promise it will never happen again. But for now, you need to be checked out by a doctor. When Terrence found out what happened yesterday at the pub, he was furious, and he chewed everyone out on the phone this morning."

"Listen, do me a favor and reassure Terrence. Tell him I'm fine and I'll be there on Monday. I won't flake out on him, so he doesn't need to worry. And there's no way I'm spending my Sunday in the emergency room. I refuse to spend hours just waiting to be examined. I'm absolutely fine. Goodbye, and thank you!"

Suddenly, his eyes harden, and all I want to do is crawl under the covers. It's not the best protection against the anger that flashes across his face, but right now, I don't see any other option.

"Either I drive you to a doctor, or I drag you to the emergency room, or..."

And then, he gives me the most lustful smile I've ever seen, a cross between desire and defiance.

"Or I examine you myself. Your choice!"

"Wh… What? Have you lost your mind? Dream on! Go and leer at someone else!"

I'm trying hard to keep my anger from exploding, but suddenly his words have made it extremely difficult… even if my body has decided to go rogue and betray me shamelessly. If there was ever any doubt about the effect he has on me, the frissons I get at the very thought of feeling his hands on my skin are living proof.

Hey! Hormones! Cool it! Stop screwing with me, okay?

My three wishes right now:

One: die

Two: die, but after one last coffee

Three: die, but after one last coffee and one kiss with Matt

In any order, obviously.

His firm, uncompromising voice brings me out of my reverie.

"Okay, kitten. For your information, any examination would be purely medical. Don't go imagining anything else. Nine years at army medical school, plus four years as a military doctor in an armed conflict zone and two years working for Doctors Without Borders have made me perfectly qualified to conduct a simple examination. So if you'd kindly stop making a fuss, maybe we can focus on your problem and do what's needed to take the edge off your pain before you drive me crazy! One more thing: I'm not in the habit of taking advantage of vulnerable women to get them into bed. They are all entirely willing and much less ferocious than you. So rest assured, your virtue is safe, even if I am ready to accept the challenge of making you scream for different reasons," he says, his eyes drilling into me.

I don't think he could have given a more effective speech to stop me in my tracks. Flabbergasted by the information he has just flung in my face, I struggle to process it all.

So, that's nine years, plus four, plus two… and if he went into the military when he was 18, then that makes him… Dammit, I've never been any good at math. Uh, 33. He's 33 years old. And… shit, what did he just say?

To preserve my sanity, I decide to ignore that last part.

It's for the best!

4. Doctor Freestyle

After a good five minutes of gaping stupidly under his unyielding gaze, I finally give myself permission to move, trying to regain my composure. I frown and take a deep breath.

"Uh… I don't know if this is such a good idea…"

Exasperated, he pinches the bridge of his nose and sighs noisily. "Charlie! Enough already! It's Sunday, finding an emergency doctor wouldn't be difficult, but we'd have to go all the way over to the other side of town. And if you go to the emergency room, there's a good chance we'll be spending our whole day there. So unless you've got a better idea, I think I'm your best option at this point!"

What am I supposed to do? Lift up my t-shirt and say "ninety-nine"?

"Alright! Alright…"

"Good! So, can you stand up?"

He holds a hand out to me and helps me extract myself from my bed. Without letting go of my hand, he positions me so that I'm standing between his knees.

This whole situation is too surreal. I can't deal with it, so I stare fixedly at the floor. Just the touch of his skin against mine is enough to make me tremble.

"I'm going to examine you. I'll try to be gentle, okay? I don't want to make the pain worse. I'll need you to lift your t-shirt up to your chest," he tells me gently.

I silently obey, scrunching up my t-shirt just under my breasts. I try to stop myself from blushing, but I can feel the heat rising in my face, and my breathing quickens. This is silly... this isn't the first time I've been examined by a doctor. But shit, this is Matthews we're talking about. I don't even dare look at him. He must be able to see how embarrassed I am. With my t-shirt up, I can see a huge bruise on my left side. The color goes from deep blue to a sort of dirty purple. Matt's eyes seem to be struggling to contain his fury at the extent of the damage caused by my run-in with Miss Bimbo.

"Relax, kitten. It's going to be fine."

His hands are unbelievably gentle as he places them on either side of my hips and pulls me closer to him. The heat of his palms on my bare skin instantly sends frissons shooting through me, giving me goosebumps that he could hardly miss. The sparks in his eyes are unmistakable, and that almost imperceptible wry smile only serves to confirm that he's enjoying the effect he has on me. I curse myself for the hundredth time for letting my blasted body betray me. Still, Matt continues his examination in silence, letting his powerful hands glide over me like a couple of feathers. I am staggered by his expertise. He observes me attentively, his brow creased, evaluating the damage, turning me a little from side to side. He asks me to breathe...

"Well, it doesn't look like you've broken or fractured anything, but you'll still need an X-ray to be sure. All the same, that's a pretty nasty bruise you've got there. Do you have a medicine cabinet around here?" he asks, gently pulling my t-shirt back down.

"Umm... wh... yes... Uh, it's in the bathroom."

He strides smoothly out of my room, and I hear him talking to Chloé.

No! What was I doing? What an idiot! "Umm... wh... yes...." Anyone would think I don't live here! Hey, get a grip, or you're going to earn yourself a dunce's cap!

In less than a minute, he's back with his hands full: arnica, bandages, bottled water, ibuprofen. Very efficient!

"I'm going to put an arnica dressing on the bruise, and you're going to take ibuprofen for the pain. But perhaps you'd like to shower first?"

Yes, yes, yes, and I'd like you to scrub my back, and... Knock it off, hormones!

"Yes, of course, but you don't need to wait around for the sake of a bandage. I'm sure you've got better things to do. You've already done enough, thanks. I'll be fine now."

He moves in very close, slips his right arm around my hip, leans towards me and murmurs in my ear, "You have no idea what else I can do for you. Don't think you're getting away that easily, kitten! I've got all the time in the world. Come on, shower time! Go, before I escort you in there myself... Although," he goes on with a massive grin, "that does sound like a rather tempting plan for a Sunday."

Warning! He needs to shut up! Now! Withdraw your troops immediately! Let's get the hell out of here!!!

"Umm, it's okay. I think I can manage a shower by myself. I won't be long."

I politely extract myself from his arm and make my way out of the bedroom, quite shaken, noticing as I go that he has invited himself to stretch out right in the middle of my bed. That's all I need! A string of dirty images flutter through my mind. Him on top of me, him naked, him naked from the back, him naked from the front. Him na...

Stooooop! I'm losing it completely. This shower is going to have to be cold!

◎ ◎ ◎

Aaaaaaah. Oooh, that feels good!

The hot water trickling over my skin (yes, hot, I'm not a masochist) revives me. The fog that I have been living in since my rude awakening disperses, and the knots in my muscles melt away. There's nothing better than a hot shower. Well, actually, plenty of things are better... but I've decided not to think about them for now.

After about ten minutes, I force myself to leave the stream of hot water and grab my robe. I take a moment to observe my impressive bruise. Wow. That must have been a really hard punch! I get the feeling I'm in for a tough week at work. I slip on my lingerie: black lace shorties with a matching camisole. Then I put on some black leggings, a black tunic sweater with an asymmetric slit neckline that shows off my shoulders and slips down one arm a little, and my sneakers. The perfect outfit for a difficult morning after.

When I return to my room, Matt is still lying on my bed, with his arms crossed behind his head, observing the trompe-l'oeil painted on my ceiling: a sky scattered with clouds, and the sun's rays filtering subtly through.

He looks at me curiously and raises one eyebrow before he speaks. "That painting is really well done. I've never seen such a... soothing fresco. Was it your idea?"

"Actually, it's one of my paintings..."

Caught by surprise, I can't help over-explaining, trying to hide the fact that I'm losing my senses at the sight of him lounging around on my bed. "The sky is one of the few things that brings you into the moment. Just one glance is enough to feel it, and yet it's so unique and shifting. It's not unlike our feelings. It can be foggy or clear, gloomy or bright, reassuring or threatening... The fresco contains two cycles: day and night. I flecked it with phosphorescent paint: when night falls, you can see the starry sky."

Matt seems genuinely surprised by my revelation. His eyes are wide as they move from my face to the painting and back. For a moment, he stares at me, astonished, then he is overcome by the need to express his admiration. "Woooow! You paint? You did this? You're incredibly talented, Charlie. You amaze me more and more every minute. Do you exhibit your work?"

"No, not really. It's more of an outlet for my emotions. It's... personal."

"You should! You're really astounding."

His eyes linger on me, then he gets up and pulls me close.

Pinned like a butterfly by his gaze, I feel completely exposed.

"Right then, operation bandage! Lift up your sweater!"

This time, I don't protest. I can feel his warm breath on my neck. Even though he's behind me, I can sense his eyes on me, scanning every reaction. He puts the bandage on with expertise and immense care, his nimble, precise gestures demonstrating his medical skill. When he's finished, he slides my sweater back down. Then, without warning, he kisses my neck. The kiss is long, hot, and sensual… so soft that a sigh escapes my throat before I can stop it. Now that… that was anything but medical. *Oh my God!* This guy is temptation incarnate!

I pull away before I lose control entirely. When I turn around, he flashes me a smile, biting his bottom lip with a mischievous expression that makes me dizzy.

"Done!" he announces innocently, as if nothing has happened.

Tomatoes, apples, cherries… they should all give up now. The redness record is mine! "Thanks… but what was that?"

"What?"

"That kiss!"

"You're too old for candy after seeing the doctor, don't you think?"

He'll drive me to my wits end. He's impossible. And the effect he has on me is much too dangerous.

Quick check-up:
Stress: sky high
Brain: still missing
Hormones: dancing freestyle

Great!

Matt hands me the bottle of water and a pill. Why does he have to be so irresistible?

"Swallow, beautiful," he says, not even bothering to hide the innuendo he has carefully crafted to make me blush and falter again.

This guy is toying with me openly and shamelessly! I swallow the pill and give him a withering look, but it only makes him laugh even more. How dare he! He's enjoying driving me crazy!

"Right, I'll let you get some rest. You need it. See you soon!"

With a wink, he turns and leaves my room.

What the hell just happened? I let myself flop onto my bed, where Matt was just minutes ago. His scent lingers on my sheets, and I can't help but revel in it, breathing it in deeply. I go over the morning's events in my mind, trying to detach myself from the pleasure that his skin has sparked in me. While I am lost in thought, Chloé runs in and throws herself onto the bed next to me.

"You survived, then?"

"I'm not sure!"

I can't hide my confusion from her. She knows me too well, and she can read me like an open book.

"Sorry about the coffee. Feel like watching a movie?"

"Absolutely!"

As we often do on a Sunday, we snuggle into the sofa among the pillows and watch a few good movies. She gets out a pile of Blu-rays and we pick out *The Crow*: one of our regular choices. It's Brandon Lee's last movie, and it's really dark (the main character comes back from the dead to avenge the murder of the one he loves). It's the darkest love story I know.

When the front doorbell rings, Chloé leaps up and goes out into the hallway. I see her coming back a moment later, with eight enormous cups of coffee and an equally enormous smile. "There is a God!" she announces.

"Huh? What's going on? Did you order all that coffee?" I exclaim, my zest for life suddenly rushing back.

"No, not me, sweetie! But there's a little note with your gift, and the delivery guy told me it was all paid for."

I hope a few cups of coffee will satisfy your caffeine craving and lift your mood a little.

You can put your claws away now.

See you soon, kitten,

Matt

"Care to explain? That guy is a God! What are you doing?"

"Uh... No! That guy is anything but a God! He's so arrogant!"

"No, he's meeeega sexy!"

"That guy has got issues!"

"That guy has a prize-winning butt and he gives out coffee for free!"

"That guy is... toxic!!!"

"Exactly what you need! Choke on him!" she exclaims, laughing so hard she can hardly breathe.

"Chloé! Have you no boundaries?!"

"No sweetie, none whatsoever, and you should know that by now! It's about time you moved on," she says, getting control of her breathing again and taking a more serious tone. "It's been two years, Charlie…"

5. Evening Consultation

Monday, 1:30 PM

I've been waiting on this X-ray for over four hours already. And I'm pretty sure I know what the result will be, since Doctor Matthews has already checked.

I can think of better ways to start the week. Actually, I really ought to thank him. He behaved like a perfect gentleman. Well, if you ignore the fact that it was his floozy of an ex who beat me up! And the fact that he took advantage of the situation to steal a kiss... Yes, actually, it's all his fault. I'm in a terrible mood, and I have no desire to humor him. Luckily, my darling Chloé isn't around to read my mind, or she'd stop me at the word "desire" and tell me to loosen up already.

"Miss Moreau, you're fine, everything is okay, blah, blah, blaaaaaaaaaah."

A whole morning wasted... to hear that!

Back in the apartment at around 2:30, Chloé has left for work, so I allow myself a well-deserved nap, since I missed out on my last two lie-ins.

I wake up around seven in the evening and get ready to start work at nine. When I walk through the door to the Green Country pub, my four colleagues swoop down on me like vultures going in for their dinner.

Were they hiding behind the door, or what?

I put my bag down, look at each of them in turn, and suddenly notice the concern in their eyes.

Tommy is first to speak. "Hi, Charlie. What did they say at

the emergency room? Terrence told us you were having X-rays this morning."

"How are you feeling? You're not too badly hurt, are you?" Chris asks.

Sam and Lucas scrutinize me carefully, checking to see that I look okay. Sam puts a hand on the back of his neck, looking uncomfortable.

"It's okay, guys, calm down, it's just a couple of bruises. Nothing serious."

"Yeah, well, it should never have happened! Do you hate us for it?"

I stare at each one of them in turn, and I can see that they are torturing themselves over the attack. They need to chill out!

"Hey, cut it out, guys. Everything's fine! You're not to blame for what happened. Honestly!"

"We should have done a better job of looking out for you," Lucas says, frowning.

"It happened so fast that nobody could have prevented it, so stop feeling guilty or whatever! I'm not at all mad at you."

Terrence appears behind me, wraps a strong, affectionate arm around my shoulders and asks me to follow him into the little office where he interviewed me for the job just a few days ago. Suddenly, all my confidence vanishes. I had almost forgotten that I will need to explain what happened on Saturday night to my boss. I try to decipher his thoughts from the expression on his face, but he's not giving anything away. I start mentally preparing myself to fight for my job.

"Come in, honey, sit down."

"Thanks, Terrence. Listen, I'm sorry. I—"

"Stop right there! You're the one who needs to listen, Charlie. On Sunday morning, I happened to find out that Selena assaulted you on Saturday night. Aside from the fact you've got a split lip, someone who was there told me you hit the table really hard as you fell. So I sent Matthews to see you. There are often fights in this establishment, but I will never accept one of my employees, male or female, being attacked while they're doing their job. As you will have realized by now, we're like a family here. And you're part of that family now."

"Thanks, Terrence, but honestly, I'm fine! Matt did drop by and bandaged me up until I could get an X-ray. Everything is okay. I just need to look after my bruise. There was no need to send him over. It could have waited a day!"

"That's for me to judge, sweetheart! The other thing is that I won't be around this week. Will you be okay? Are the guys treating you OK?"

"Oh, uh... Yeah, they couldn't be nicer. They've really looked after me and made me feel like part of the team."

"Brilliant! That's all I needed to hear. Well then, good luck this week, good luck with the boys, and see you on Sunday, kid."

He gets up and leans over, his massive frame casting me into shadow as he plants two loud kisses on my cheeks, then gestures that I can go back to work. I have to say, that's the most unlikely conversation I've ever had with a boss! When I come out of the office, all my tension has evaporated. I feel reassured and supported. My boss and the rest of the team have been so kind; it really warms my heart.

The rest of the evening is calm and uneventful. The bar is quiet during the week, which means I'm able to suss out some information about Saturday's apocalyptic events. The few snippets of information I manage to glean from my colleagues tell me the following:

1. The evil ex is called Selena.

2. A customer who knows Terrence well told him I banged my head on the table when Selena pushed me.

3. Terrence phoned all four of them, ready to explode, at 7 o'clock on Sunday morning. Good morning indeed...

4. Well, no, actually, that's all. I couldn't get a shred of information about Dr. Matthews! Nothing, nada, zilch, not a peep... They all kept their mouths firmly zipped! But I'm desperate to find out more about him! After all, he did barge into my well-ordered little world, into my bedroom in fact, with no warning whatsoever!

Anyway, the evening goes smoothly until my phone starts vibrating in the back pocket of my jeans.

11 PM. Unknown number. Text message.

[Hey kitten. Still alive?

Your bandage needs changing,
I'll be there in an hour. Matt]
    IS THIS SOME KIND OF SICK JOKE?
I immediately text him back.

> [You can get that idea
> out of your head right now.
> No way are you coming here.]

Ten seconds later, my phone is dancing the salsa in my pocket again.

[Nice try… Too late, though, I'm here!]

Shit and double shit.

I slowly lift my gaze from my cell phone, and at a height of 6'3, it meets Matt's unfathomable blue eyes. All the blood in my body floods to my cheeks, turning my already pink face bright crimson. The eye contact makes my head spin. Hell, why won't he leave me alone? Normally, when I send a guy packing, he doesn't push it. So why won't he give up?

"Good evening," he says, a predatory smile sneaking across his lips.

Towering over me, he leans in, places a powerful hand on the small of my back and starts whispering in my ear.

"Nee-naw, nee-naw."

His audacity makes me stiffen, and he seizes the moment to reward my immobility with a delicate kiss on my cheek, really dragging his little game out.

Uh, I mean, how should I…?

How could I not be stunned by such confidence? This guy likes playing games! He's a master seducer. I can't even move a muscle. Dammit! This is getting ridiculous! I've got to get a grip, right now.

Oops… there's just one thing I forgot over the course of these past five minutes… Four pairs of eyes are burning into us, not even bothering to hide their curiosity. Sam, Lucas, Tom and Chris stand there gaping, not missing a second of the action.

> *State: poor, must try harder*
> *Heart: riding a rodeo bull*
> *Legs: useless*
> *Brain: in serious trouble if I ever find it*

"Matt, hi, you shouldn't have..."

He stands there staring at me, gaging my reaction. Then, suddenly, his eyes crinkle in the corners. "Kitchen!" he says.

"Huh? Noooo! No way!"

Sunday's improvised striptease was quite enough for me, thank you!

"Yes, right now!"

Before I can protest again, he takes hold of my arm, pulls me to him, picks me up effortlessly, and carries me into the next room. He places me on the edge of the metal countertop, opens the little bag he is carrying on his back, and gets out what he needs to change the bandage.

And I flip out. "What the hell is your problem? I'm not some toy you can carry around and dump wherever you like. Is anyone in this shit pit of a world ever going to respect what I want? If you want some broad to play with, go and find your Selena or any of the countless other girls lining up for the job. But just remember one thing: I am not available for that role!"

I don't even know if I'm angry or offended. All I know is that I'm confused; my eyes sting with tears. Again... Why am I so oversensitive?!

Why?

Why can't I be more detached?

Why do I always feel unsettled in his presence?

Why, when I feel his eyes on me, do I feel like there are barnacles feeding on my brain?

Why does he keep pushing?

Lost in my useless attempts to make sense of it all, I don't see him approaching. His index finger lifts my chin, his thumb wipes a tear from my cheek, and his warm voice breaks the silence that has fallen between us. "Charlie, I'd like you to listen to me. Can you do that, please?"

His serious tone throws me for a moment, and I nod. When I raise my eyes to meet his, what I see confuses me deeply. There's no trace of mockery, no judgment... just great sincerity.

"We work in the same place. I've been here much longer than you, and I've been around the block here. I won't pretend I haven't. Now, I won't let you take the blows for mistakes I may have made. I mean Selena, of course. In no way do I want to hurt you or cause you pain. I just want to get to know you. That's all. So maybe… could we be friends? Is friends too much to ask?"

"Friends? Nothing more? Just… friends?" I repeat, strangely disappointed beneath my relief.

"Yes, kitten! Friends."

The idea of being friends with Matt is reassuring. Except that it will be pure torture, because dammit, he's not just thrilling to look at, but he also has a brain and he uses it. What would Chloé say? Oh yes… "Let go! Live a little!" Friends… That's a good compromise, right?

"Okay, Matt, just friends!"

Surprisingly, at this moment, I was convinced he would respond with a victorious grin. But no, his smile is incredibly tender.

"Lift up your sweater!" he adds with a wink.

After this bizarre exchange, and once the bandage has been changed, we go back into the bar where my four colleagues are deep in conversation—no need to ask what about! In the end, this evening hasn't been such a disaster. Quite the opposite. I'm relieved at how things have turned out. I can get on with my job in peace.

6. Deal or No Deal

At the end of my shift, I pick up my bag and say goodbye to the guys. I'm about to leave when Matt catches up with me. "Did you drive here?" he asks.

"No, I walked. I wanted to enjoy the nice weather! Anyway, I don't live far away."

Once again, I can tell from his expression that he's not going to take no for an answer.

"I'll give you a ride!" he says. "You're not walking the streets alone at 1 AM."

"Thanks, but there's no need, Matt, I'm a big girl, I'm used to it."

"Well, I'm not!"

"What do you mean you're not? You're not a big girl? Really?"

His face hardens for a second, then he gives me a devilish grin. He undresses me with his eyes, lingering deliberately on the more generous curves of my anatomy. "I'm driving you home, kitten," he sighs, "and friends or not, nothing is going to stop me proving what this big girl has in her pants, you, insolent thing, you!"

Embarrassed and amused by his response, I blush violently.

We leave the pub together, with the boys' eyes burning into us, and I walk alongside him until we get to a magnificent black pickup. "Wow, is this yours? It's enormous!" I exclaim, obviously impressed.

"You mean my 4x4, right?" he answers, with the kind of cheekiness only he can bring to such a situation.

I almost choke on his reply. Instantly, I am bright red again. You could easily mistake me for a beetroot.

"I'm joking, Charlie! Come on, get in! Do you need help?"

I swallow a laugh at his teasing, climb into the vehicle, and settle into the plush passenger seat. Matt starts the motor of this amazing ride, then turns to me.

"Before I take you home, there's somewhere I'd like to show you," he says softly. "Would you like that? But we can leave the moment you've had enough."

"Have you seen the time? Couldn't we go tomorrow, or…?"

"No, tonight! Please," he insists, pouting sulkily in a way that makes me almost melt into my seat.

"Is it far?" I ask.

"About 15 minutes from here, if we drive slowly. Is that a yes then?"

"Well, okay," I agree, "but I don't want to stay too long, I'm exhausted!"

"As you wish, milady."

It's only a short drive, but I must have dozed off, because when I open my eyes, Matt is leaning over me, brushing a thumb across my cheek. We have stopped, the motor is running, and we are parked by a pond with a huge weeping willow hanging over it. The thin branches stream down like a waterfall around us.

"What the—"

"Shh. Come with me!"

He gets out of the car and comes around to open my door, with a blanket rolled up under his arm. God, he's sexy! I let him lead me, his hand taking possession of mine. I don't say a word. It's so peaceful here, so… just, wow, what a gorgeous place! I close my eyes for a moment, breathe in the sweet air, and listen to the leaves rustling. Everything here is idyllic. When I open my eyes, Matt is looking at me strangely. He is sitting on a blanket at the foot of the willow tree, with his back against the trunk, one leg stretched out, and the other knee up with his arm resting on it nonchalantly…

My hormones are up in arms! I hate this!

"Come and sit with me," he says, his eyes glued on me as he gives me the most charming smile I've ever seen.

As I go to sit down, he spreads his legs, positions me between his thighs, and wraps his arms around me. The feeling of his muscular body against mine makes me stiffen.

Wow! Just the touch, just the scent of him…

We said "friends," dammit! Friends, and nothing more!

As if he can read my mind and wants to calm my escalating discomfort, he starts rocking me slowly, with his head in the curve of my neck. All my resistance slips away, and I give in to this healing moment. I close my eyes, making the most of every second of comfort he offers, of this peace I have not felt inside me since it was violently snatched away two years ago. Without me realizing, my fists clench at the memory, so hard that my nails dig into his palms. Before I can open them again, Matt weaves his fingers through mine, not saying a word. He keeps rocking me as the tears threaten to spill over once again.

"Look!" he whispers suddenly.

In the air above the pond, a strange ballet has begun. Dozens of fireflies have appeared and are dancing in front of us, darting around and skimming the water… I've never seen anything so magical! And it's Matt who is responsible for this wonderful moment. I'm speechless.

Suddenly his soft mouth is on my shoulder. Infinitely tender, he isn't kissing me; he's tasting me, his lips sliding up towards the curve of my neck, leaving my skin slightly damp where his tongue has performed its own nimble ballet. Oh hell! The fear comes bubbling up. Gnawing and merciless…

He stops my thoughts in their tracks, pulling his lips away and tipping me over to one side, while keeping me in his arms. This guy is a real enigma. His eyes burn right through me.

"Sorry," he says, in a voice that implies he is anything but. "I… I couldn't help myself. I don't mean to be pushy."

"No… I mean… It's not your fault. It's okay. It's me…"

"Please Charlie, talk to me," he pleads, his voice both gravelly and silky at once.

But I can't manage a single sound: all that comes out are tears, spilling down my cheeks, betraying my pain.

"Charlie! Who did this to you?"

Tightening his arms around me, Matt slides one hand

behind my head and clamps me to him, against his heart, rocking me again to calm the sobs that are escaping from my throat. He gives me a little kiss on the forehead, without saying a word, just comforting me so that I can finally let it all out…

◎ ◎ ◎

When I feel his mouth on mine, I open my eyes. I can see the first hint of daylight on the horizon. I am still nestled in his arms, under the blanket.

The memory of his kiss immediately fills my mind. Was it a dream? No, I don't think so. I can still feel my skin tingling from the touch of his lips.

"Morning, kitten! We fell asleep. It's 5:30 in the morning. We should probably get you home," he whispers.

"Oh shit! Uh, yeah, okay."

I get up, feeling a little uncomfortable. We said friends, yet we've just slept together under the stars.

Good sense and willpower: zero.

And I fell asleep crying. Classy! Okay, let's do this in order:

One: Don't ogle Matt as I wake up.

Two: Did he kiss me?

Three: Dig a hole and bury myself in it forever.

Four: Did he kiss me?

Five: I said, "don't ogle Matt!"

Noticing me shuffling uncomfortably, Matt takes the blanket from my hands and folds it. In one step, he covers the distance between us, cups my face between his hands, and says, "Hey, is everything okay, Charlie?"

I raise my eyes and see him trying to soothe me with his gaze. I nod, and we head for his pickup.

Fifteen minutes later, we are outside my building. Like before, he gets out to open the door for me, and before I can register what's happening, I find myself with my butt perched on the hood and Matt between my legs.

He's totally unpredictable. His masterful yet gentle manner surprises me every time. Oddly enough, his natural authority doesn't frighten me, because he is so careful with me, and it's becoming harder and harder to keep my cool...

"It's time to sum things up!" he announces, tapping the bridge of my nose with his index finger. "One: I really enjoyed last night, and I'm here if you ever need to let it all out again. Two: whenever you feel ready, you can tell me, and I'll be there. Three: I would recommend you don't panic over a few kisses! Four: I'll come and pick you up at noon! See you then, kitten!"

With his little speech finished, and everything neatly laid out and wrapped up, he lifts me off the hood, plants a kiss on my forehead, and pushes me into the foyer of my building, then leaves.

Argh... HELP! Can anyone explain to me what's going on? Because right now, the only thing that comes to mind is the music from The X-Files!

A mirage, or a hallucination? I'm still not sure what has happened these last few hours. Somehow, clearly on autopilot, I manage to get back to the hallway outside my apartment. I am fishing robotically in the bottom of my bag for my keys, when suddenly, the door swings open to reveal a haggard-looking Chloé. She almost scares me to death.

Oh my God!

Now I'm in trouble. Big trouble! Chloé won't let this slide. No way. She's going to harass me, torture me, pick apart every little thing I say until I give in and tell her all the details. The day is decidedly off to a bad start. And it's not even six in the morning! "Uh... You're up already?"

"Quit messing around Charlie. Are you going to explain? I've been frantic with worry! You are aware that these days we have a gadget called a TE-LE-PHONE! It's very handy, it lets people talk to one another! Okay, I know maybe that's not your thing, but was even a text message too much to ask? What's going on in that brain of yours, anyway? A foam party? Do you have any idea how worried I've been? Where the hell were you? And more importantly: WHO WERE YOU WITH?"

The sands of time have started shifting in my head. I could stone a donkey to death with soft figs by the time she stops her braying. So, I go ahead and give in. "Sorry. I didn't think to call. It was late. Also, I wasn't doing so great, and, well... Matt and I fell asleep, and we only woke up half an hour ago, and there were fireflies, and—"

"Whoa! Stop right there! Say that again! You spent the night with Matt? Did I skip a page? Spit it out before I squeeze it out of you like lemon juice!"

One of the things I love about my friend is that she can go from hysterical to compassionate at the speed of a galloping unicorn. I think my face must be saying "please, just kill me now," because she suddenly wraps her arms around me and gives me an enormous hug.

"I was so worried! Come on, a double coffee for me, and a triple for you!"

Then I tell her everything. I spill out a wave of information, from our "just friends" pact to the hot kisses that destroyed it. From the fairytale beauty of the place to the emotions that are overwhelming me. Chloé's eyes get wider and wider as she registers the details of my impromptu escapade with Matt.

"Woooow!" she says, grinning widely.

"Mmm... yeah. But I don't know if..."

"If what? If your panties are ready to say thanks? You've got a free ticket to this red-hot guy, who is ready to give up sleep just for the pleasure of spending a few hours with you, who behaves like a perfect gentleman, and who is happy to play tissue to your tears. You know what? Let go a little! Relax with a friend and stop overthinking it. At least make an effort to get to know him before you give him the brush-off once and for all! You're having fun together, not getting engaged. Learn to live again... and I am ordering you to get some sleep, then go and eat with him. You even have my blessing to eat *him* if you like!"

"We're not quite there yet."

"Yeah, well, get moving before your hormones sue you for neglect."

I can't help but smile at all her efforts to get me back in the saddle. I drink my coffee, then collapse on the sofa and curl into a ball with a huge, soft, fluffy cushion in my arms. When Chloé comes over to cover me with a blanket, I turn my eyes to her anxiously.

"You'll be fine, sweetie. I won't let anyone hurt you: if

anyone so much as thinks about it, I'll puree their balls and eat them for breakfast," she tells me gently, before I sink into a deep sleep.

7. Finger Food

When my cell phone beeps, I resolve to open an eye. 11 AM…
I need to get moving and jump in the shower! I quickly dart my
eyes over the message.

[I'm hungry!!!
There in 10 minutes. Matt]

> *This guy is insane! What is he running on? Rocket fuel?*

Sound the trumpets of the Apocalypse! I'm going to throw
myself into the shower so hard I might hurt myself! Eight minutes
later, I am desperately wriggling into my jeans. I dance like a worm
on a hook, because jeans and damp skin are not a particularly
advantageous combination.

Diiiing dooooong, the doorbell rings.

Barefoot, with my hair dripping wet, I open the door to
a devastatingly tantalizing Matt. It's just not possible to be that
attractive! Wearing an angelic smile, he takes in my every detail
from head to toe, making no attempt to hide how pleased he is to
find me in this state.

Irritated that he has once again caught me half-dressed, I
can't hide my exasperation at his amusement. "You said noon!
Are you in the wrong time zone or something?"

"I told you, I'm hungry," he says, taking me in his arms and
giving me a long kiss on the cheek.

This simple, innocent gesture sends electric shocks right
through me. To be honest, I'm angrier at my body for reacting this
way than I am at Matt himself, who is clearly aware of my internal
battle. "Don't you ever sleep?"

"Stop bellyaching and step on it!"

"Okay, I'm coming, I'm coming," I cry, jamming my feet into my sneakers.

I don't really give much thought to where we are going to eat. It's like I'm leaving myself in Matt's hands, letting him take me to a little restaurant by the sea. He's a weird guy. In fact, I know almost nothing about him, about his life (except his taste for country music and his skill for finding the perfect, muscle-hugging clothes for his Herculean body, of which he seems completely unaware). Apart from this, all I know is what he has told me about his past career.

Once we are seated on a shaded terrace, he hands me the menu, smiling with his elbows on the table.

"I hope you're hungry!"

"Yes," I begin, "but obviously not as hungry as you, judging by your sudden inability to tell time."

Matt's deep laugh makes my stomach flip flop. His smile is so gorgeous, his butt is so gorgeous, and... I'm losing track...

"So then, kitten, what do you want to talk about?"

Huh? I don't know! Why is he asking me? I'm useless at making conversation, and right now, my brain is bouncing around.

Note to self:
make an effort to improve my communication skills
check list welcome

"I don't know, but since my ability to communicate seems to be somewhat limited at the moment, if you feel like starting, please be my guest!"

"Great. Then we'll start at the beginning! I'm from Texas originally, my mother was French and my father was Texan."

"So that explains the accent? Texas. Now I know why you like country music so much!"

He rewards me with a charming smile and continues his discourse. "I lived there until I was seventeen. That was the year I lost my parents in an accident, and I came to live in France with my uncle, with whom I had spent my summers. When I was eighteen, I joined the army. You already know the rest."

A thousand questions spring to mind, but get caught in a traffic jam behind my lips. I hang back, preferring just to let him talk about what he wants to talk about. I'd hate to stick my foot in my mouth. And anyway, I don't want to talk about my past. I don't want to spoil this moment.

The rest of the meal is nice. As the time slips by, I realize that I feel good around him. He's attentive and fills the gaps whenever I don't know what to say. We even taste each other's food. Two friends sharing a meal. You might almost think we'd known each other for years! I don't know what to make of it... We have a kind of instinctive connection, and to my great surprise, I feel comfortable.

When the waiter brings our deserts, my sweet tooth doesn't go unnoticed. Even my eyes are watering at the sight of my *crêpiteroles*: vanilla ice cream wrapped in silky crêpes and doused in melted chocolate and whipped cream.

Unable to resist temptation, I plunge a fingertip into the whipped cream, but before I can even taste this airy treat, Matt has grabbed my wrist, and my finger is in his mouth. His eyes penetrate mine as he savors my dessert and, studiously slow, his tongue rolls around my index finger, which he sucks lightly before letting it go.

"Mmm, delicious!" he purrs with a dazzling grin.

OH MY GOD!

I can't cope! My hormones are out of control! I'm hot, sooo hot. Even the ice cream in my crêpes is hot! Since when do friends suck each other's fingers?! Was there some fine print in our "friends" pact? My mind wants me to keep control, and my body wants me to relinquish it entirely. This guy is smooth: he is systematically breaking down the barriers I have built around myself. Distracted by my desperate internal battle, I jump when he asks me if I fancy a walk on the beach, making it sound like the most natural question in the world.

It's been so long since I've walked on a beach. And at least I can be sure that if I catch a fish, he won't start sucking my finger. I nod in agreement, and we finish our meal. As soon as we are out of the restaurant, Matt takes me by the hand, our fingers intertwining naturally. Surprised, I initially try to pull my hand away, but his firm grip and the serious look he gives me at that moment put a stop to my escape attempt. His eyes are full of tenderness, with an undercurrent of astonishing determination. I have to confess he's won me over, and I give in to this sensation of safety. I even have to admit I like it.

We pick our way through the crowd, which is especially dense at this time of year, strolling through the arcades full of summery boutiques. We play around trying on sunglasses, hats, and other seasonal accessories, each more ridiculous than the last. The season's ludicrous fashions leave us gasping for breath between fits of laughter.

A quarter of an hour later, we come out into a little alley leading to the beach. The perfect view is accompanied by a sweet, salty sea breeze. The glimmering water stretches out as far as the eye can see, waves lapping sensually at the shore, stirring up white foam. We sit on a nearby dune to take off our shoes, and run towards the shoreline like kids, impatient to paddle into the sea. As we charge towards the water, we can't stop laughing. Matt starts running after me, catches me, and whirls me around in his arms.

When he puts me gently back down on the ground, my thoughts are all over the place. How long has it been since a man has made me laugh so much? I don't even know... I suddenly feel water hitting my back, interrupting my musings. Within seconds, we're in the middle of a water fight, tourists looking at us as if we'd lost our minds. When we stop, both of us are soaked through. Nothing could have prepared me for such an intense day. I've even surprised myself, letting go of the restraint that is so deeply ingrained in me.

Exhausted by our frolicking, we head back up the beach and flop onto the warm sand. Like it's the most natural thing in the world, Matt rolls onto his side, props himself up on one elbow, and pulls me close. He has one hand on the small of my back, and his gaze penetrates mine. With his eyes fixed on mine, he moves closer, infinitely slowly, closer and closer to my lips. Nothing else matters: not the people, not the rising wind, not even the fact that I've forgotten to breathe. His lips brush mine incredibly gently, caressing the corners of my mouth, his breath warm, showing unbearable self-control. Then, his tongue slips into me, looking for mine, rolling around it in an erotic ballet, ever more intense and intimate. When his teeth imprison the edge of my bottom lip, the electric shock it sends through me scorches everything in its path.

After I don't know how long, he moves away, his cautious eyes locked on mine.

"Matt, I…"

"Don't start panicking again, kitten."

"Says the one who suggested that 'just friends' pact in the first place!" I remind him. "Since when have friends sucked each other's fingers… and tongues?"

"Since one of them was convalescing! I call it 'cuddle therapy!'" he adds with a wink.

Totally thrown off course by our embrace, my heart struggles to slow its beat. It is thudding in my chest, accompanied by my halting breath. I feel feverish. What about all my resolutions? His touch makes them melt away like snow in the sun, and I don't know whether I'm coming or going… "You're impossible! Shouldn't we be going? I need to dry off and get dressed for my shift this evening."

When we get back, Matt drops me off in front of my building around 6:30 PM, giving me a chaste little peck on the cheek. Surprisingly, the apartment is empty. No sign of Chloé. She's normally around at this time. I go into the bathroom and set about getting all the sand out of my clothes. After a long shower, I am glad to put on something dry and clean. Looking at myself in the mirror, I notice that my cheeks are pink, and the few freckles that come out every year are visible. Damn sunburn.

○ ◎ ◎

The rest of the week goes flawlessly. I even learn that Chloé has hooked up with Sam. Well! It doesn't exactly surprise me, given the looks those two have been giving each other since I've been working at the pub. All the same, my roommate was curious about my little trip to the seaside, and I had to fill her in the next day.

I'm not seeing Matt this week. He's busy rehearsing and writing a new song. That leaves me plenty of time to analyze the evolution of our budding relationship. He has the irritating habit of wearing down my defenses. It's annoying. At least, I think it is. Am I really ready to go along with this ambiguous pact that has us tightrope walking along the boundaries of friendship? Am I ready to turn the page?

The deep thoughts of a disturbed brain.

Turn the page! Yes, but...

If life really were a book, I would have chosen the story.

In the end, I spend hours tidying up the mess in my head. Chloé tells me that she and Emily will come to the pub on Saturday night for a drink. Cool, I love having them around!

We make small talk until she blurts out, "And is everything going well with Matt?"

"What do you mean, 'with Matt?' We've said we're friends…"

"You're not fooling me with your little act, Charlie. Talk about smelling a rat: your story is infested with them!"

Shit!

8. Shake It for Me

I opt for a relaxed outfit on Saturday night: white blouse, jeans, and my Converse sneakers. I really need to be comfortable during my shift, given how crowded it's going to be tonight.

Like every Saturday, people start streaming in. Matt, already in place for the show, gives me a wink and a disarming smile. Good grief! How he manages to make my head spin like this is beyond me.

The first notes fill the room: "That's My Kind of Night."

The ecstatic crowd floods onto the dance floor. The atmosphere is electric, with everyone dancing wildly. I almost have to wrestle my way through them. Every time I get near the stage, I feel my entire body melt. He keeps fixing his eyes on me, smiling, and thrusting his hips. How am I supposed to hold a tray full of glasses when my hands are shaking from Matt's incessant teasing?

Chloé and Emily arrive a little later, and they sit at a table slightly out of the way, quickly becoming engrossed in the show. The atmosphere is buzzing tonight.

Terrence tells me to take a break, and I seize the opportunity to join my friends at their table. The next song, "Shake It for Me, Girl" drives the room wild, and the girls pull me out onto the dance floor.

I glance over at Terrence, and he nods his permission. Then we're off, shimmying for all we're worth. It's only when the revelry becomes deafening that I turn around and see Matt on the dance floor, walking towards me.

Oh my God, what is he doing?

He keeps singing into his head mic, and stands facing me, with his hands on my hips, his own gyrating suggestively as he makes me sway with him. Phew, it's hot in here! I'm not sure I can take any more, but I can't resist, and I let myself go with him on the dance floor. I lock onto his powerful shoulders and feel his hands tighten their grip on my hips, expressing his contentment. I'm not sure how many beats my heart skips. I feel exposed, yet protected. Just another aspect of the unbelievable effect he has on me. His breath caresses my neck, making me shiver—I even feel a bit dizzy. I pull back slightly and realize that he can see that I'm afraid of being kissed in public, even if some part of me, deep down, wants it. When the song is over, his eyes plunge into mine and he kisses my cheek with a strange, satisfied smile. As I watch him walk away, I realize that even though he didn't kiss me on the lips, everyone here knows what's going on now since he has just virtually advertised how much he wants me. He takes his place on stage again and makes an announcement. "This next song is a new one!" His eyes settle on mine. He languorously adds, "I hope you like it!"

Then he starts singing, "Every Time I See You."

I glance over at Emily and Chloé. They are both staring at me, dumbstruck.

"What?"

"Charlie, this song's for you," Emily gasps.

"Yeah right, we're friends, that's all!"

"Friends, ha, yes, of course you are!"

I dismiss her with an impatient wave of my hand. I'm embarrassed and uncomfortable now, and I promptly ask them not to hassle me about what they just saw. "Will you knock it off already with your insane theories? When there is any news, you'll be the first to know, so please just let it go for now!"

They both smile knowingly and sip their drinks. "Right, I'm off back to work."

I head towards the bar and Lucas comes over to talk to me."Umm, Charlie, we've got a problem..."

"What's going on?"

"Look over there!"

I look towards the entrance and my eyes fall on Selena. Is God out to get me or what? "I just need to steer clear of her, it'll be fine."

"That might be tricky, given that she's seated in your section."

"Oh shit! Okay, don't sweat it, I can handle it that harpy: so, plan A: I'll serve her like any other customer, and if plan A doesn't work, I've still got 25 letters left in the alphabet…"

Lucas bursts out laughing. He hands me the order for her table, and I walk confidently towards my serving area.

I put the drinks on the table, keeping my attitude as professional as possible, but apparently Selena has no intention of leaving me in peace. Her furious eyes burn into my skin, and she addresses me with all her usual hostility. "You, waitress, keep away from Matt. Don't touch him. He's mine. You're just a waitress. A pathetic little waitress."

Who does that skank think she is anyway? I'm not going to let some middle-class witch look down her fake nose at me! "Okay madam. What else would you like with your order? Lessons in good manners? A drink to celebrate your property deed? Oh no, sorry, silly me! Matt has moved on! How hideous for you!"

"You little slut. Are you calling me hideous?"

Now I've really had enough. I refuse to be treated like this. "Are you permanently stuck in stupid mode or something? I didn't say that! But, if you want this pathetic little waitress's opinion, well, no, you're not hideous, your face just needs op-ti-mi-za-tion!"

As I turn my back, I feel liquid in my hair. Thick, red and sticky, it runs down my neck and shoulders, onto my white blouse… Damn! That evil little…! How dare she throw her Bloody Mary all over me?!

I whip around and give her a murderous look.

What does she think this is? A sitcom? I'll get her for that!

Well, when I've managed to scrape off the thick layer of foundation, makeup, and all the other muck she uses to hide her foul face, that is. I hear Chloé's voice over the uproar the scene has caused, telling Matt to get me out of here. I am ready to leap at Selena, when I feel Matt's powerful arms wrap around me and lift me up. I wriggle like a kid being put in a stroller, trying to free myself from his grasp. He puts me on the ground and asks me to calm down, but it's official, I've snapped! "That bitch!"

If she wants some, I've got plenty for her. When I've finished with her, she'll be lucky if she can move! Matt is talking urgently to Terrence, and Selena seizes the opportunity to escape Sam's vain attempts to control her. She pounces on me, brandishing her glass!

Suddenly, I remember what my coach taught me: right, left, side step, roundhouse kick, elbow to the face, and… Ooooh, damn that was a good one!

The bitch is down for the count. I'm nice but don't push me.

Score so far:
Rocky: one
Self-control: zero
Professionalism: Uh… needs work!
Technique and tactics: Excellent, I'm making good progress!
Immediate goal: Start looking for another job, again…

Before I can say anything, Matt firmly grabs my hand and leads me out of the pub. He pulls a ring of keys out of the pocket of his jeans and puts one of the keys into the door next to the Green Country entrance. His face is closed and his lips are pressed together in silence. I can't even open my mouth, and to tell the truth, from the furious expression on his face, it's best that I don't. In front of us is a long corridor with a tiled floor, and at the end of it, a staircase leading upwards. At the top of this is a big, black door. "Where are we?" I ask.

I look up at him and suddenly realize what's happening.

"My place!" he answers, his voice a growl and his face unreadable.

He opens the door and turns to me. "Get inside!"

"No!"

"Get inside!"

"No! What are we doing?"

"C'mon, Charlie, are you kidding me?!"

He kneels down so he is level with my hips and slings me over his shoulder easily, like a sack of potatoes. He goes into the apartment and violently slams the door shut. He walks halfway across the massive duplex with me hanging over his shoulder, my head dangling, pounding him on the back, trying to get him to put me down. When my feet are finally back on the ground, I am in the middle of a room the size of my whole apartment. Initially, I am speechless. Then my thoughts start firing off in all directions.

Who is he really? What does he want? Why am I here?

Panic invades me, uncontrollable and insidious. An icy wave of fear fills my body. I don't know what to do. My hands start to shake. I feel my throat tighten and tears fill my eyes. "So?" I suddenly explode, screaming at him. "What is this? What's your problem? What are you going to do now? Huh?"

He looks stunned. His eyes widen and he frowns, holding up his hands before he speaks. "Whoa, whoa. Wait. Calm down, it's because—"

Without even giving him time to continue, I step back sharply and raise my voice even louder, enough to snap my vocal cords. "Stop! Don't even think about coming near me!"

"Hell, Charlie, I'm just trying to—"

"Trying to what? Have me at your mercy? Why have you brought me here?"

He gestures towards me, still staring, taken aback. "Shit, calm down, I…"

This time, the tears are out. I can't hold them back.

"No, I will not calm down!" I holler. "What are you playing at? We've known each other, what, a week? Do you think that gives you the right? Nobody, do you hear me? *Nobody* will ever play with my life or control me again. And nobody will tell me how I should behave, goddammit! I'm not one of your fashion victim, silicone-filled groupies! I've taken enough shit to last me ten lifetimes, so get off my case! I've been trying to dig myself out of it all for two years now: two years of shrinks, trying to convince myself that this lousy life is worth living! Two long years when the only place I have felt safe is at home, with Chloé, keeping the outside world at bay! So I'm sorry if I gave your precious little doll what she had coming to her, but believe me, I don't regret it!"

Rooted to the floor in front of me, Matt wipes a hand over his brow and tries to make some sense of the flow of information spewing from my mouth.

"Shit! If you only knew how little I give a damn about Selena! I just want you to talk to me, Charlie. I want you to explain, so I can understand."

He holds a hand out to me, but I recoil abruptly, not noticing that the Bloody Mary all over me has dripped onto the floor. As my heel hits it, I slip over backwards, and the only thing I can find to grab onto is a shocked Matt, whom I pull down with me, falling heavily. By some miracle and thanks to what are obviously fantastic reflexes, he doesn't fall on top of me. He is holding himself up on his palms. His hands are on either side of my head, his face dangerously close to mine.

"Talk to me..."

At this point, all the fight goes out of me. His closeness, the soft feeling of his breath on my cheek... it is enough to make me lay down my weapons. I am entranced by the concern in his eyes. With him here, so close, I feel exhausted but safe, and I decide it's time to reveal my past.

"Something... something bad happened to me. I broke up with my ex and he took it badly. He... he showed up one morning at 5 AM, armed and furious. He strangled me, threatened me, then held me prisoner in my home for a whole day so that I would take him back. I had to play along to make him think he was getting what he wanted. Once I had reassured him, he left and I called Emily. I was terrified. She came immediately and took me to the cops to report what had happened. After that, I moved in with Chloé. My ex left town. It turned out he was involved in some shady stuff, and my complaint drove him away. There, happy now?"

My face is drenched with tears again as I relive this painful memory. My voice is a croak. My stomach twists sickeningly.

"Oh, no! The son of a...!"

Matt studies me, his face just inches from mine. His gaze is penetrating, searching deep inside my eyes. Initially he looks furious, then just bewildered.

I see his jaw clench, muscles tensing, teeth grinding. He seems to be lost in thought, and I can't help hungrily taking in every detail of his square, distinguished face. Disoriented, I lose my grip on my incoherent, jostling thoughts. I am overflowing with contradictory emotions. I feel like I'm teetering on the edge of a precipice. Drawn by the desire to let myself fall into the void below, but fiercely holding on to my senses. Is he going to kiss me? Shit… What do I do if he kisses me?

He stands up effortlessly, cutting my thoughts short, and knots his fingers around mine to help me to my feet, all the while keeping his eyes on mine. How is he so charismatic? Even with spots of Bloody Mary on his T-shirt, he's still alluring…

Unexpectedly, tenderly, he tucks a sticky lock of hair behind my ear.

"You are seriously in need of some tickle therapy…"

"Tickle therapy? Wait. What?"

"Are you always this nervous?" he says, trying not to laugh. "Relax. Haven't you ever heard of tickle therapy? It just means relaxation through tickling. And I am your therapist. So get yourself into the bathroom, run yourself a nice, hot bath, I'll bring you some spare clothes, and while you are in there, I'll make you a little meal. Then we can watch a good movie, and eat marshmallows and various assorted other junk. Sound good?"

"No. I'm not going to take a bath at your place! That's ridiculous."

"Oh right? And traveling across town covered in sauce is any less ridiculous? Unless you love organic tomatoes so much you want to display them proudly in your hair? Or even better: you're going to launch a new eco-grunge trend! Or maybe—"

"Stop! Enough already. Okay, I'll take a bath."

He gives me a dazzling smile, proud that he's gotten his way. God, he can be so annoying… and sexy.

"I'll go find you some clothes. Be right back."

I take the opportunity to look around while he's in the other room. I have to admit that the decor is tasteful. Furniture with a brown patina finish, white walls and powdery beige curtains. The atmosphere is very cozy and very… masculine. An enormous corner sofa sits in the living room, with a magnificent silvery-gray, long-pile carpet in front of it. I hardly dare move lest I dirty his apartment even more.

When he gets back, he gives me some clean clothes: a T-shirt, boxer shorts and a jacket. "They'll be much too big for you, I'm sure, but at least you'll be comfortable. When you're done, I'll wash and dry your clothes, and you can have them back."

He really is full of surprises. He has everything under control, and yet he still has that enigmatic charm. It could come off as bossy or unpleasant, but from him, it doesn't at all. Quite the opposite, actually. I just want to let him guide me. I want to lean on someone. I want to savor these arms in which to rest for a moment, and that is exactly what Matt is offering me. I take the pile of clothes and he points me towards the bathroom. "Thanks, Matt."

"Go on! Go splash around. I'll make some food."

9. What You Really Fancy

I slip into the bathroom, and what I see leaves me at a loss for words. This room is crazy gorgeous!

It looks like something out of a specialist spa magazine! A massive, anthracite-glazed corner Jacuzzi bathtub takes pride of place on the left side of the room. Above it, a set of metal shelves exhibit an array of bath products. Once again, Matt's taste leaves me speechless. A black marble, half-moon sink stands in front of me, and to the right of it is a walk-in shower covered in small pebbles in different shades of gray.

I run the water and let myself be cradled by the soothing warmth. This bathtub is massive! My feet don't even reach the end. I start carefully washing myself to get rid of all the sticky sauce.

Suddenly, I hear music in the room. Speakers on the wall are playing a jazzy tune that finally helps me completely unwind, and before I know it, I am savoring this moment of fabulous relaxation.

Once I am feeling completely refreshed, I slip on my host's boxers and T-shirt, smiling at my reflection in the mirror. I am lost in the clothes, which are undeniably far too big. I throw on the jacket and join Matt in the living room. The aroma in the air makes my mouth water. God, is he a Michelin chef or something?

As he sees me walk in, he looks up and gives me a spellbinding smile. His eyes twinkle naughtily at the sight of me. "Yeah, I know, they're too big, I…"

I shuffle around on the spot, horribly embarrassed, not knowing how to act.

"They're perfect," he answers. "You're adorable! Come and sit down."

I join him, still a little uncomfortable, and sit at the table. Only then do I notice that he has changed: he is wearing an American university sweater. He has also put on different jeans, darker than the ones he was wearing earlier. He looks absolutely breathtaking.

"Do you like fish? Bream fillet with sautéed potatoes…"

"I'm impressed! Do you enjoy cooking?"

Feigning embarrassment, he nods and fills our plates. The fish is unbelievable: melt-in-your-mouth, perfectly seasoned… Heavenly! "Oh wow! This is insanely good, Matt! You just keep surprising me. Any other hidden talents?"

He smiles and looks at me naughtily. "Oh, you can't even imagine, kitten! Would you like some more?"

Oh shit… This guy is like a piñata—full of tasty surprises.

"Uh… N… no. No, I'm fine, thanks. It was delicious."

He keeps looking at me intensely, and I have to fight to avoid melting under his gaze. Images flit through my mind: his hands on me, stroking me sensuously. This has to stop! I feel my cheeks going pink and heat rising all through my body. Why won't my brain leave me in peace? The traitor!

"You look uncomfortable. Anything wrong?"

I struggle to swallow, my throat is dry. This is so awkward. Can he tell what I'm thinking? He radiates such confidence that I don't even dare raise my eyes in case I see my desire reflected in his. Instead, I change the subject, in order to avoid sliding down a slippery slope. "Uh, no. Nothing at all. I'll help you clear the table."

We get up, carrying the plates into the kitchen, another jaw-dropping room. I'm not surprised he likes whipping up tasty little dishes here! Functional, high-tech, spacious: perfect for a budding chef. A counter separates it from the living room, with lamps hanging above it from four metal cords. The minimalist space goes perfectly with the rest of the decor. I couldn't imagine a better design. I observe Matt out of the corner of my eye while he is busy putting the dishes into the stainless steel sink. I can't believe I'm here with him. When he turns around, there's no mistaking his smile. He caught me checking him out. Dammit!

He doesn't comment. He just stares back at me, raising his eyebrows in satisfaction, but he doesn't look pretentious, more like... intrigued. As if I'm not the only one with more questions than answers.

"Feel like a cup of coffee?" he says.

"I'd love one, coffee and I have been faithful and passionate companions for many years."

"Does a guy need to be caffeinated to stand a chance with you?"

"Huh? What?"

"Don't worry, I'm joking!"

He winks, grabbing two cups, and starts the percolator. We take our cups and return to the living room, putting them on the coffee table.

"I'm going to get some snacks. You make yourself comfortable."

I snuggle into one corner of the sofa, glancing up as he comes back carrying bags of chocolate-covered marshmallows. Right this second, he looks like a little boy breaking the rules, ready to binge on sweets. His natural, simple aura disarms me. He's still just as gorgeous!

"I think we're fully equipped for the evening! Just give me a minute to take a quick shower, and then we'll watch some movies. Look in the cabinet underneath the TV: see if you can find any DVDs you like the looks of."

I watch him walk out of the room, and suddenly, my evil inner voice makes itself heard.

Would it be unseemly to unzip his pants to see what I really like the looks of?

No! Shut up! I close my eyes and focus on choosing something from the wide selection of Blu-rays in the cabinet. Let's see: *Avatar, Legends of the Fall, Harry Potter* (the full collection), *The Lord of the Rings* (again, the full collection), *Thor, Footloose, E.T., The Godfather...*

Varied taste... but good! All the best movies and oh, oh, oh... *The Crow*, my favorite! Does he like it too? My thoughts are interrupted when he comes back into the living room. His wet hair hangs down in front of his eyes in a few places. He is bare-chested, with lounge pants slung low on his hips. Scandalously sexy! He's irresistible! My hormones start doing somersaults in my stomach. Does he even know the effect he has on me? He pulls on his sweater and walks towards me. "Find anything?"

"Yeah, nice collection! There are some real classics in here. *The Crow* is my favorite movie. I don't know how many times I've seen it, but it never loses its impact."

"It's one of my favorites too!"

He puts in the DVD and sits on the sofa. I position myself carefully at the other end. It's safer here!

"What are you doing over there?" he smiles.

"Getting comfy."

"I don't bite, you know."

He reaches an arm out and slides me towards him, positioning me between his legs.

"There, much better!"

Pushed up against him like this, with his body behind mine, I give in and let his body heat warm me.

The movie starts, and Matt grabs the package of marshmallows, takes one and offers it to me. Just as I am about to take it, he pulls his hand away. "Open your mouth."

I tentatively obey. He brushes the marshmallow against my parted lips, then delicately places it on my tongue. I let myself relax into him, keeping my eyes on the screen. His hand moves from the back of the sofa to my stomach, cocooning me in his arms. A strange feeling of safety envelops me, destabilizing me, but I might as well just admit it: I don't have the strength to fight or to question my decisions. I'm happy here like this. And for now, I have no desire to spoil the moment.

Absorbed in the movie, I can feel his breath on my neck, slow and warm. His thumb is softly caressing my skin through my T-shirt. A cloud of butterflies takes flight inside me, sending frissons throughout my body. I occasionally feel his gaze settling on me, as if he is watching my every reaction to his innocent caress.

◎ ◎ ◎

When I feel him lifting me up, I open my eyes in surprise. I fell asleep! Cradled in his arms, I let him carry me to his bedroom, where he gently lays me on the bed. "I have to go home, Matt."

"No, you need to sleep!"

"I'll sleep at home."

"I'm afraid you can't. I forgot to dry your clothes!"

"You forgot? Seriously?"

"You might say that, yes. Go on, kitten, sleep," he urges gently.

My mind is still foggy, so I stop resisting and let myself sink into slumber.

◎ ◎ ◎

I jolt out of my sleep full of strange dreams.

What?! Where am I? Oh yes, I'm at Matt's... Matt's? Shit! What time is it? I glance at the clock on the bedside table. It's just after 4 AM. The room is almost entirely dark, lit only by the pale moonlight filtering through the curtains. All I can make out is the shape of Matt lying beside me. He's so... impressive, even when he's asleep. I let my eyes linger on his face, his torso—uh—his naked torso. Naked? I am wondering if he's still wearing his pants... when my thoughts are interrupted by his silky voice, "Enjoying the view, kitten?"

I hide my face under the covers, too mortified to speak. I feel him moving next to me. He slowly takes the duvet and slides it off, forcing me out of my hiding place. Propped up on one elbow, he looks at me inquisitively and smiles. "Why are you hiding?"

He leans towards me and moves a lock of hair aside with the tip of his index finger, which he trails down to my jaw, before cupping my face in his hand. His thumb brushes over my slightly parted lips. My body reacts instantly. Electricity shoots through me, and I see his tongue flick over his bottom lip. He moves forward carefully, watching for even the tiniest signal from me, then places his lips on mine.

His kiss is tender and deep, his tongue penetrating me, savoring me, seeking mine to dance a sensual ballet. He gently tames me, running his tongue over my swollen lips, nibbling them, one hand tangled in my hair at the base of my neck. He pulls me closer. His scent is intoxicating, and my heart is beating wildly, slamming hard against the inside of my chest as if it is trying to escape.

My brain makes a futile attempt to remind me of my goal of abstinence, but the intense fire of this kiss silences it once and for all. I feel my body slowly unwinding, unraveling, enjoying everything about this moment. His mouth drifts cautiously behind my ear, covering me with its heat. I sigh and hear him moan with pleasure. He continues his exploration along my neck, and his hand slides down to the arch of my back to bring me even closer, pinning me against him. Breathless from our kisses, he undresses me with his eyes, before his gaze locks onto mine. Panting, trembling, I have never felt so alive.

"At this rate, I'm not sure I'll be able to control myself. Damn, you drive me to distraction, but I don't want to rush you. I want you to trust me. I don't want you to feel afraid of anything. And most of all, I want you to feel ready."

"Matt, we said we were just friends. And…"

"We can be more than one thing."

I have no idea where all of this is headed, but I have to be honest with him. However hard it is. "It's been a long time since I… well, you know. I… I'm sorry, I—"

He silences me with the gentlest of kisses. "I forbid you to apologize, got that? Therapists orders! Your emotions are healing!"

I give him a big smile instead of an answer, which seems to satisfy him. He gets up and puts on his pajama pants, which it seems he took off to sleep in just his boxer shorts. "Are you getting up?"

"No, but your therapist has a massive erection and he needs a cold shower!" he answers with a wink.

I burst out laughing, and he leaves the room, laughing with me. God. He's got a really mischievous side. How does he do this? Every moment we spend together chips away at the walls I have so diligently built around me, and I can feel my defenses crumbling. Suddenly, I realize that I walked out of work. I didn't even go back before closing time or talk to Terrence. Shit! How is he going to react? He was cool about last time, but I doubt I'll be so lucky again.

I am mulling it all over and over in my mind when Matt comes back. He is still wearing the same hint of a smile, but he tilts his head inquisitively. "What's on your mind, kitten? If you keep chewing the inside of your mouth and frowning like that, you'll end up looking like Jim Carey in *The Mask*!"

"Terrence is going to kill me! I'm sure of it! I haven't even been in touch since we left the bar! This time, I'm definitely going to be out of a job. I got away with it the first time, but twice... I'm in big trouble!"

"Relax, I called Terrence while you were in the shower, and I let him know you were staying here with me. He's more worried than angry. He knows who was in the wrong, and it's not you! I asked him to tell Chloé and Emily too, so relax."

I can't believe this guy: thorough, organized, and methodical! Everything I'm not. "Oh!"

"Come on, time to get some more sleep!"

He stretches out next to me, slides under the covers and wraps his arms around me. I curl into them peacefully, and he tightens his hold. Cocooned in his arms, I let the emotions wash over me. It's been so long since a man held me like this. I've been alone in my bed every night for two years. Two years of shielding myself. And somehow, he has brought me out of my shell. Without forcing the issue—just because he's... him. "Thank you, Matt."

"My pleasure, kitten, really. Now come on my angel, get some sleep."

10. Mister Boom Boom

The sun filtering through the curtains drags me out of my slumber. I wake up and stretch like a cat. The alarm clock says it is 9:15 AM, and I notice that Matt has already gotten up. Where does he get his energy? Knowing me, I'm going to traipse around all day now.

I get up and go into the living room. I can hear noises from the kitchen, where I find Matt concocting the kind of breakfast I would expect to find in a five-star hotel. When he sees me, his face breaks into a devastating smile. He takes me in his arms and plants a kiss on my neck. It's the strangest feeling: as if from the moment we wake up, we have instantly formed a little ritual as a couple. Everything feels... natural, simple, and spontaneous. I have to admit that the sensation is intoxicating, and it feels amazing.

"Sleep well? I hope you're hungry."

"Morning! Yes, very well thanks, and yes, I'm starving. You're bouncing with energy—what time did you get up?"

"About eight. Did I make too much noise?"

"I didn't hear a thing. I slept like a cat!"

"Yes, I can confirm that you even purred..."

"Huh? What? I snored?"

"No, you purred. And you're sooo sexy when you purr..."

I feel my face turn the color of beetroot. Good start: already red before breakfast!

"And when you blush! Coffee?"

"Yes, please!"

He smiles, and as we eat, we talk about everything and nothing, making the most of our Sunday morning. He tells me my clothes are dry and that he's left them in the bathroom. I go to shower and get dressed.

A quarter of an hour later, I join him back in the living room, but he's on the phone.

"Yes... hold on... I'll ask her; here she comes..."

He puts his hand over the phone. "It's Sam—he's having a barbecue at his place at noon," he says tentatively. "He's invited us. And... He wants to know if you'll invite Chloé too. All the team from the bar will be there. Do you want to go?"

"Oh! Uh, sure, but I'll have to call Chloé to let her know, and go back to my apartment to get changed."

He tells Sam that we'll be there, looking delighted, then hangs up.

"I'm glad I get to spend the day with you," he announces. "I'm going to jump in the shower. See you in a minute."

I use this time to call Chloé, who agrees almost before I've finished asking; she's not about to miss a chance to spend time with Sam. When Matt comes back in, I can't help devouring him with my eyes. Dressed in a black shirt with the sleeves rolled up over his forearms, very worn jeans, and a pair of white leather sneakers, he's just stunning. He stands in front of me, perfection in human form. I am lost in his scent, and my inner demon is stirring.

It's going to be a very trying day indeed...

It's almost 10:30 when Matt drops me off at my building.

"I'm going to pick up a dessert, then I'll swing by and get you."

"Okay!"

I run into my building, and the minute I'm inside the apartment, Chloé throws herself at me for one of her special, crushingly enthusiastic hugs.

"How are you? That was quite a beating you gave that hussy. Are you okay? Not hurt? Are you sure? And you slept at Matt's? Does he live far away? Is his place big? What did you do? Do you think I stand a chance with Sam? I really like him, you know. So tell me, did you tumble around with Super Matt? That's twice he's come flying to your rescue now. My God, that guy is any self-respecting woman's fantasy! And you're sleeping with him! I can't believe it! That's twice it's happened now. Twice he's managed to get you to spend the night with him… The guy's a genius. My idol. And—"

"Chloé! Do you need to take a breath?"

"Oops, sorry! At least answer one question, though: are you okay?"

I give her a reassuring smile and nod. "I'm doing great, Chloé. Now, I have to get changed before he comes to pick us up. He's at the bakery."

"Did you…?"

"Noooo! Not yet…"

"Does that mean you plan to? Go on, say yes… Tell me you want to get between the sheets with Mister BOOM BOOM!"

"Mister Boom Boom? What?"

"You do realize that he's the first guy in two years to knock down your defenses. He's completely demolished your ivory tower. Better than a bulldozer! He's dynamite! Hooray for Mister Boom Boom!"

I snort, unable to contain my giggles at Chloé's buffoonery. She laughs along with me, and we rush into my bedroom to choose my outfit. She opens my closet and pulls out the little black dress she gave me for my birthday. I haven't even worn it yet. The label is still attached. She thrusts it firmly into my hands. "It's perfect for today!"

"I'm not wearing a dress, Chloé! I was thinking more along the lines of jeans and a tank top."

"Yes! You're going to wear a dress, and you'll thank me later! You're not going to upset me by refusing to wear my present, are you?"

What a dirty trick, she's got me cornered! "But…"

"No buts. Get dressed, Charlie!"

I give in. There's no point trying to fight Chloé, anyway. Once she's made her mind up about something, she doesn't let up. I quickly get dressed, then put on my black ballet pumps and some light makeup. The dress is gorgeous. Simple yet elegant. Thin black straps, with a deep V neckline, it cinches in at the waist and flares out down to the knees. It has a low back with a zipper, offering a glimpse of the butterfly on my shoulder, carefully tattooed by Emily.

I find Chloé in the kitchen, and judging by her face, she is more than satisfied with the result. "That dress was made for you!"

My cell phone beeps with a message: Matt is waiting outside. We rush out to meet him. He is leaning against his truck with his arms folded, but when he looks up, his expression changes radically. I'm sure I see sparks in his eyes. He's about to say something when Chloé intervenes, "Hey there Boom Boom, how's it going?"

He looks at me, puzzled, and I burst out laughing. I give Chloé a thunderous glance, but she is happy with her inside joke and just gives me a scheming look, then starts laughing too. Matt looks confused, but his lips curl into a dazzling smile and he decides it's best not to ask.

"I don't know if I should laugh or be worried, but I'm glad to see you in such high spirits! Come on, let's go. Barbecue time!"

◎ ◎ ◎

We walk up the alley to Sam's house, chatting.

We've not even set foot on the doorstep when Sam appears, wearing a chef's apron.

"Very sexy!" Chloé snorts.

Sam is amused by her teasing and can't resist showing off, posing like a bodybuilder. "Come in! The others are already here, in the back garden."

We hug everyone hello, and Lucas serves the drinks.

There is music blaring out from the speakers in the living room: a great rock song, which encourages my four colleagues to break into dance. I am chatting with Tommy, who is busy barbecuing, when I feel a warm hand in the hollow of my back. Matt is standing behind me and pulls me close, wrapping a possessive arm around me. His lips brush my neck.

"Did I mention that you look breathtaking?"

My own breath catches in my throat. Just the touch of his lips sets all my senses buzzing. I'm just getting a grip again when Tommy wields a sausage at us threateningly.

"Whoa!" he exclaims. "You two will turn the meat bad if you don't keep your sexual tension to yourselves. Go play somewhere else. It's not nice to taunt lonely souls!"

Hooting like teenagers, we move away before he starts throwing chipolatas at us.

Soon, we are all sitting together, enjoying a beautiful day. Obviously, yesterday's little fight is a hot topic, and Chris raises a toast. "To Charlie. Our honorable Valkyrie!"

"To Charlie!" everyone choruses.

Moved by everyone's attention, I can't help but sigh. Matt instantly spots my turmoil.

"Everything okay? You seem... overwhelmed."

"Yes, I'm just amazed that people who hardly know me care so much, when my own family isn't capable of it!"

He softly comforts me, stroking my back with the flat of his hand, and looks at me curiously. "I haven't told you about my family yet..."

"Do you want to?"

"Well, you might as well know. We're quite a small family. Just my father and my mother. I'm an only child, but there's always tension between us. They've never understood me, and to tell the truth, they've never really tried." I pause, rolling a pebble around under my foot. "When I was attacked and I told them I had reported it, they immediately asked me what I had done to provoke it. They were convinced I was responsible for what happened. So there you have it... rather than trying to console me, they were indifferent to my sadness... again. So I cut all ties with them."

"Shit, Charlie, that's crazy! How could your parents be so despicable?"

"Now can you see why all of you caring about me like this touches me so. It makes me feel like I've found a family."

He wraps his arms around me tenderly. "The Green Country does have a family spirit!" he whispers in my ear.

Later that afternoon, we play an improvised game of volleyball, and the atmosphere is just fantastic. The boys are so fun... comical, even. Their clowning knows no limits, and everyone just about ends up on the floor in stitches.

Exhausted after a particularly frantic match, we sit down for a drink. Matt settles into an armchair and pulls me onto his lap. The discussion gets livelier. We talk about the pub, motorcycles, girls, and music. Matt's hand sneaks onto my thigh, softly caressing it.

The butterflies, which had settled, take flight again.

"Are you having a nice time?"

"An amazing time, I must say. Everyone seems so close…"

"They are. We all are. And you're the first girl to join the team."

"Seriously? There's never been a girl working at the pub?"

"No, never."

"Oh! And why not?"

"None of us were so sure about having a girl at the pub. We don't mean to be sexist, but you've seen how a night can get out of hand. We all have to vote on any potential waitress. Until now, none of the girls who applied got unanimous approval. Terrence was never happy with them. You're the first one to pass the test."

"Do you know why?"

"No, we never managed to get him to tell us, but you could ask him sometime—maybe he'll be willing to tell you."

Tommy comes back, his arms piled high with beers.

"Drinks!" he announces.

I am about to stand up to get us some beers, when Matt's arm closes around me, pulling me to him.

"No. Wait," he whispers.

Suddenly, I feel a dangerously swollen bulge in his jeans, pressing against my butt.

"Neigh, neigh," he murmurs.

"Dammit, Matt! Can't your inner horse control himself?"

"My inner horse is desperately trying to control himself, with your butt pushed up against him, kitty!"

My face is hot, and his words make it impossible to contain a sigh of arousal. As if to lessen my torment, he showers feather-soft kisses on the bare skin of my back.

His lips barely brush my skin at all, but the delicate, attentive caress gives me goosebumps. With every frisson that washes over me, I feel his husky, hot breath on my neck, making a sound almost like a purr of desire.

"Sleep with me tonight…"

11. Ode to a G-String

We leave the merry band at around 6:30. Sam sees me to the door and tells me he will drop Chloé off at home.

I'll believe *that* when I see it...

On the way back, I doze off, lulled by the smooth sound of Marvin Gaye filling the car. A whisper wakes me from my slumber and I realize we have stopped. Matt is leaning against his door, looking at me. "Dammit, I fell asleep again!"

"I'll forgive you," he smiles.

"Where are we?"

"Halfway between your place and mine! You never answered me... Will you sleep with me tonight?"

"I don't know if..."

He reaches out an arm and lifts my chin with his index finger.

"Do you want to? Answer me. Do you want to sleep next to me tonight?"

"Yes."

His mouth moves towards mine, murmuring his thanks. "Right, let's go."

As we walk into his duplex, I feel awkward. This started off as a friendship, but it's moved so quickly. I must say that, from the moment we met, he has made me feel things that are above and beyond. What kind of spell has he cast on me? I'm mystified.

He throws the keys on the counter and turns to me. The atmosphere in the room is suddenly drenched in desire, and a ferocious anxiety grips me tight. It's been so long... Captivated by the intensity of his gaze, I feel my breath quicken. He walks towards me, his feet padding silently across the room, until he is towering over me, his eyes still locked on mine. I lean against the wall, and he places his hands against it on either side of my face, surrounding me with his body. Heat pulses through me, flooding my veins and accumulating deep in my abdomen. I feel like I am in a delicious trap. Although my fears about what might happen next are very much at the forefront of my mind, desire takes the upper hand. His kiss is intense, deeply intimate. He uses his tongue to toy with me, catching my lips between his teeth, sliding his mouth down my neck. My legs almost give way under the weight of his lust. His hands come to rest on my hips, then slide down my butt cheeks. He grabs them and presses his body against mine.

"God, you drive me crazy…"

He leans down and lifts me up, kissing me the whole time. I instinctively wrap my legs around his waist, so that we are locked together, and he carries me slowly to his bedroom.

He puts me down and gently spins me around. Sweeping my hair aside, he carefully begins to unzip my dress, letting it slide to the floor. His mouth is on my neck. Still behind me, he slips off his shirt and presses himself against me. His hand strokes my stomach, sliding up to my neck, where my pulse is throbbing.

"You're divine…"

His voice is husky, hot and heavy with want. I abandon myself completely, letting him guide me along pleasure's path. He knows how much trust I am placing in him. He lays me down on the bed, his fingers running over my body in curlicues, decorating me with his desire. He sensually slides the straps of my bra down my shoulders, caressing the lace with his fingertips, and then pauses as he reaches the valley between my breasts. Each of his movements is precise and focused as he scans my eyes for silent consent. Then he skillfully undoes the hook. Freed from their restraint, my bare breasts are pert and hard with lust. He cups them in his powerful hands, tasting my erect nipples. The contact sends an electric shock right through me and my body arches violently, submerged by this exquisite wave which elicits a groan of pleasure from my throat.

"Oh! Tell me to stop, or I won't be able to make myself…"

"Don't stop, Matt. Please…"

I hear him moan with pleasure, and his tongue works its way downwards, sliding down my belly. He slowly slips my thong off and kisses the tops of my thighs, his hands caressing my knees, parting them tenderly so that my world is there for him to see. There is nothing now that could stop our bodies from becoming one. When his mouth gently touches my bush, I fall into a deliciously dizzy spiral. I'm wet with desire, and his caresses feel unbearably glorious. He gently licks my clitoris, titillating it, tracing circles around it, sucking it so that my flesh swells between his lips. He tastes me deeply, sighing with pleasure, savoring my intimate nectar. I am trembling violently, and he uses one arm to hold my hips firmly. He suddenly slips two fingers into me, still tormenting me tenderly with his tongue. My whole body convulses as his fingers penetrate me skillfully, caressing the warmth inside, exploring my luscious hollow.

"Come, angel, come for me…"

I feel the orgasm building, burning through me, and I can't stop myself shouting out his name. "Maaaatt!"

Just as I'm about to peak, he penetrates me more deeply with his fingers, and a liberating cry explodes from my lips. I am shocked by the power of my pleasure, and my body is tingling all over. I am breathless, weightless. I feel like I'm floating. Matt looks into my eyes, covering me with his body. Propped up with one elbow on each side of my face, he kisses me with infinite tenderness.

"I can't get enough of you. Ready for round two?"

Still breathless from what I just experienced, I bury my hands in his hair, pulling him into another kiss. His body, glued to mine, presses greedily against me. His hips are rocking and his hard cock, ready to burst out of his jeans, leaves no doubt as to what he has in mind. He gets up, releases it from its clothing and gets a condom out of the drawer, placing it on the pillow. He turns to face me, naked, magnificently shameless, and positively stunning. His impressive erection leaves me wide-eyed, speechless, and suddenly nervous… with good reason: he's huge! Sensing my trepidation, he lies down next to me, keeping his movements careful and slow.

"Are you panicking?"

"Um, yes, well, a little."

"Trust me…"

He tucks a stray lock of hair behind my ear and leans in to kiss me softly. The kisses soon become hot and hungry, stoking the fire within me. He rolls onto me, grabs my hands and lifts them over my head, his fingers intertwined with mine. The movement of his hips against mine is hypnotic, and my breath is shallow in my chest, echoing his. As his tongue caresses my lips, one of his hands slides under my butt to pull me up against his throbbing cock. His mouth catches one of my nipples, which he carefully takes between his teeth, then sucks eagerly. His caresses set all my senses ablaze, and I let out a moan, trembling with lust. With one hand, he grabs the condom, rolls it down his huge erection, and holds himself at the entrance to my most intimate place.

"Now I'm going to slip inside you… all the way."

As good as his word, he gently slides himself into me, then with a thrust, fills me entirely. I feel my muscles contract around him, wrapping around his manhood. He stays like that, not moving, just kissing me and giving me time to get used to the swell of him inside me. I grip his shoulders and hook one leg around him, and he starts thrusting in long strokes, controlling every single inch. His eyes don't leave my face for a second, attentive as he is to every trace of pleasure. He starts moving faster, thrusting deeper into me, multiplying my pleasure. His thumb is playing with my clitoris again, which tips me over into roars of ecstasy. Drowning in sensuality, we abandon ourselves to each other, letting our orgasms unite in a simultaneous explosion of bliss.

Then we lie there exhausted, trying to catch our breath, Matt is on top of me with his face nestled in my neck. We gradually recuperate, and I feel Matt's soft caress on the curve of my breast.

He lifts his face towards mine, softly stroking my hair. "Are you okay? I… I wasn't too… rough?"

The deep concern for my feelings in his eyes brings tears to mine. He has just presented me with the most exquisitely erotic moment of my life. A tear trickles out. I'm overwhelmed by emotion… "It was amazing, Matt, I couldn't have asked for better."

◎ ◎ ◎

Music tickles my ears, pulling me gently from the peaceful sleep that has embraced me. The space next to me in bed is empty. Matt is clearly more of a morning person than I am.

I jump out of bed, throw on one of the shirts that are hanging on the armchair next to his closet, and go in search of my panties. Dammit! Where could they be? I desperately shake the bed sheets: nothing. So I kneel down, hoping to find them under the bed, but no. My panties are nowhere to be found. I can't see myself strolling into the living room with it all hanging out... But I don't want to go rummaging in his closet for emergency boxer shorts either. I head towards the door and hear him humming, strumming his guitar. Quiet as a mouse, I open the door, but he looks up at me and indulges me with an illustrious smile. "Uh, sorry, I didn't mean to interrupt. It's... Can I listen?"

"Good morning, kitten! You'll hear it on Saturday. It's a new song. Tell me, are you planning on coming out of the bedroom, or are you going to hide behind that door all day?"

"Umm, no, uh, actually... I... You haven't seen my panties by any chance, have you?"

He puts his guitar down next to him, stands up smoothly and walks towards me, smiling, pulling my panties out of the back pocket of his jeans and swinging them under my nose. "Hey! What are you doing with my underwear?"

"I needed inspiration. I didn't want to wake you up. You were dead to the world! So I... improvised!"

"Improvised? With my panties? I hate to think what you're going to call your song... What's it going to be? 'Ode to a G-string?' 'Lament of the Lost Lingerie?'"

He bursts out laughing, grabbing me by the waist and lifting me up against him. "Nothing quite so charming. Let's just say that last night gave me plenty of inspiration. I wanted to get things down in writing as soon as possible, while the feelings were still fresh. Thank you... for last night... for trusting me."

His mouth seeks mine, and with calculated slowness, he uses his tongue to play with my lips, instantly unleashing the horniness within. When he puts me down, my legs are still trembling from the effect he has on me.

"I waited so we could have lunch together!"

He spins around and heads into the kitchen, where I join him a few minutes later.

"My shirt looks fantastic on you."

A timid smile flits across my face and I blush with pleasure. How can I find the words to describe him right now? Bare-chested, wearing only worn jeans with the top two buttons undone. Hot? Thrilling? "I thought I might borrow it. I didn't bring any spare clothes. You don't mind, do you?"

"Mind? About what? The pleasure of seeing you half naked, wearing my shirt? I've had worse problems, believe me."

I smile like a love-struck teenager. I like it when he teases me. It's delightful. I can't wait to hear his new song. As we finish eating, my eyes drift to his guitar. Before I can stop myself, the question is out, "Do you earn your living from music? Is it your career? Or just a passion?"

"Let's just say I make a certain amount from it, but it's not all I do. Music is mostly a way to let off steam. It is a passion that brings in some cash, yes, but it's not my only source of income."

"What do you do?"

He tries to hide it, but I notice an almost imperceptible hesitation before he answers. "Oh, nothing that exciting: I work with companies in different sectors, and I manage various businesses, investments, public relations…"

He gets up and walks around the table to join me. With a swift flick of his foot, he spins my stool around, locks his steely blue eyes onto mine, and gives me a quick smile.

"I have a question for you too."

"Uh, okay, go for it."

"Do you see any reason not to continue what we started last night?"

My brain does a triple jump, and my inner thighs tense at the thought of what might be coming. "I'm pretty sure we finished last night…"

"No, I'll never be finished with you!" he utters.

He lifts me up and carries me towards the bathroom, pushing open the door and putting me down gently. Standing in front of me, he starts undoing the buttons of his shirt one by one, his forehead pressed against mine. Slowly, he kneels down and slides my panties all the way down my legs, inch by inch, kissing my thighs. Then he stands up, steps out of his jeans, and leads me over to the walk-in shower.

He presses a hidden button near the side. The first notes of Radiohead's "Creep" drift through the air, casting a surreal atmosphere around us.

The hot jets make our skins slick and he pins me against the pebbled wall. With our eyes locked together, we gaze at each other for so long that his penetrating gaze ends up hypnotizing me. I feel awkward, but I'm dying to show him how much I want him. I shyly rest my hands on his muscular chest. I am burning to touch him. I let my fingers wander over his tanned skin, his perfectly defined muscles firm and sculpted. My eyes devour every inch of his body: a body so perfect that any artist would kill to paint him. His mouth captures mine, tasting my lips carefully. His tongue frolics around mine with his special brand of playful sensuality. The kiss melts me, intoxicates me.

Still fueling my desire, he moves slowly down my body, cupping my breast in one hand, letting his tongue linger on the nipple, teasing it with his teeth and sucking it deliciously.

Every caress is perfectly executed. My libido has been locked up too long, and it is raging to be free. I struggle to keep my breathing steady. Like the conductor of an orchestra, he leads us, sets the tempo, slows us down… He's a maestro of passion, and I abandon myself to his touch. I submit entirely and blissfully to his every whim, letting him play with my body. Patiently, he continues his symphony of pleasure, moving lower and lower, leaving a hot trail down my stomach. Now, his hands have a firm hold on my butt cheeks. Kneeling in front of me, he slides a hand under my thigh and lifts it onto his shoulder.

"Hold on to the edge of the alcove, and put your other leg on my other shoulder."

He supports me, his hands under my butt so he can easily maneuver me, and I find myself with my back pinned against the wall, thighs on his shoulders, wide open for his mouth to savor. There are sparks of lust in his eyes, which burn with the promise of my divine agony. And the very idea sets me ablaze. With him, I am discovering pleasure, audacity, complicity, trust. With his eyes glued to mine, he runs his warm tongue over my most intimate and sensitive parts. Time seems to be moving in slow motion as he devours me. My body jolts with the shocks he triggers.

He closes his eyes and keeps tasting me, clearly enjoying my torment.

He excites me, taking his time, penetrating my lips, burying his tongue deeper like he could never have enough of me, sucking me greedily as if someone might take this treasure from him at any moment. Cocooned in the wetness of the shower, we are both panting, our breathing almost as loud as the music. I feel an unstoppable wave of heat rushing through me, ready to burst. But Matt feels my trembling, and pauses, giving me a mischievous look. A smile twitches in the corner of his mouth, as he takes my clitoris between his lips once again and sucks it intensely. My pleasure explodes violently as he continues nibbling, holding me firmly against his mouth.

Dizzy and breathless, I am helpless in his hands as he gently lowers me back to the ground, then stands up so that his body can slide close to mine. He buries his head in my neck, biting my earlobe, his hot breath caressing me, his fingers exploring me.

"You're ready... I want you!"

His words increasingly arouse my desire to be possessed by him.

He pulls out a condom from the alcove, tears the packet open with his teeth and rolls it easily down his erection.

He lifts up one of my thighs and penetrates me slowly. My muscles close around him, contracting and making him roar. He fills me entirely, stretching me intimately with his impressive proportions. He waits for me to adapt, for my body to accept his powerful presence. When I relax, he starts a long, in-and-out movement, covering my neck with kisses. I can feel his jaw clenching as he forces himself to hold back and contain his more... vigorous desires. I am drunk on the scent of him, the heat of him. All of my inner nerve endings are throbbing and crackling from his carefully timed thrusts. I am amazed as I discover what it really means to give yourself to someone. He gives himself to me, and I give myself to him. Gradually, the rhythm speeds up, and he takes me with all his length, thrusting faster and faster into me with one goal: to disappear into me and find ultimate joy. My cries echo in the small space, mingling with his sighs. The orgasm sweeps us away together, his body stiffens and I feel his cock pulsating inside me, sending a thunderbolt of pleasure through our bodies. We abandon ourselves to the moment, breathless and satisfied.

"God, Charlie... You drive me wild!"

He picks up the bottle of shower gel and starts soaping me delicately, prolonging this moment of intimacy.

"I have to work this afternoon," he says.

"And I have to recover before I can even think about working," I laugh.

"Shall we get dressed and I'll drive you back to your place?"

"Perfect!"

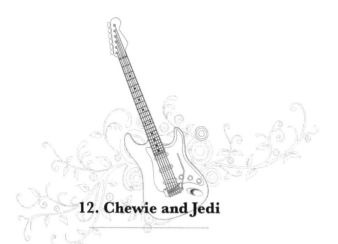

12. Chewie and Jedi

When I walk into the apartment, I think I hear a noise.

Chloé's home. Prepare for the third degree, I tell myself, smiling.

I slip off my ballet pumps and start unzipping my dress, but a deep voice stops me before I let it drop to my feet.

"Oh, shit! Charlie, no! If you carry on, I'm a dead man!"

Sam's head emerges from the sofa, his hands clamped to his face. My eyes almost pop out with shock at finding him there, half-dressed with his hair all tousled. "Shit! Sam! What are you doing in my apartment?"

"Uh, well… I brought Chloé home and I wanted to stay, but she made me sleep on this blasted sofa!"

Chloé strides into the room, a triumphant smile plastered across her face. "Just consider yourself lucky I didn't castrate you!"

I snort with laughter. Oh, that Chloé! She enjoys torturing Sam, but he laughingly takes it all in stride. Anyone would think he likes it! He stands up, pulls on his sweater, and runs a hand through his hair, trying to tidy it up a bit. He strolls nonchalantly over to Chloé, drops a kiss on her forehead, then comes and kisses me on the cheek.

"I'm off, girls, I'll leave you to chat. I'm feeling a bit outnumbered!"

He shuts the door behind him, leaving Chloé and me standing in the living room, staring at each other. Who will be the first to spill the beans? Instead, we both burst into hysterical laughter.

◦ ◦ ◦

Two hours later, we are sitting on the rug in the living room.

"So how do you feel?" My best friend asks, "And I don't just mean your post-coital afterglow!"

"To tell the truth, I feel… good. Remarkably good, even! Some of my self-confidence is starting to come back."

"Are you seeing him tonight?"

"Uh, I don't know, we didn't talk about it. All I know is that he has to work this afternoon. How about you? With Sam?"

"Sam is… in a bit too much of a hurry."

"But you like him, don't you?"

"Yeah, but I don't want him to think he's won me over that easily."

We spend the rest of the day chatting quietly in front of the TV, but I don't hear a peep from Matt.

I think about sending him a little message, but decide against it. He said he had to work, and I don't want to disturb him. Anyway, he might be in a meeting or managing a project. Finally, I resign myself to my fate. He knows how to get in touch when he's done with his work.

◎ ◎ ◎

When I get to the Green Country pub at around 9 PM, Terrence is waiting for me outside. "Come in, Charlie, let's go into my office."

His neutral voice gives me no clue to his mood, and I feel the panic rising.

Shit! I forgot I had this to deal with. I feel confused and deeply uncomfortable. I follow him in silence.

He sits down in an armchair, gesturing for me to take a seat next to him.

"Right, Charlie, I won't beat around the bush."

These words alone make my stomach churn and I shrink down into my chair. Suddenly, I am forced to face reality, and it's horrible.

"But first of all, I want to put your mind at ease: the Green Country couldn't manage without you. You've proven yourself, there's no doubt about that. And the guys adore you. I've got a tricky situation here, though. I need you for the weekend of

October 31st. We're organizing 'Green Country Halloween,' and I desperately need you to help me decorate the pub. There's no way I can ask the boys: I shudder to think what we would be in for! Of course, you'll be paid for your services! What say?"

I stare at him, my eyes bulging. This guy is unreal!

"So? Is there a problem?"

"Uh, no, well yes, but no. I thought you wanted to talk about the fight on Saturday night, so I'm just a bit surprised. I…"

"Oh, that? Wow! You certainly gave her what she had coming! Charlie, the Green Country Valkyrie! No, no problems there. Here, we like to say: 'If you're looking for trouble, you'll find it!' And that, Charlie, was the perfect example! Don't sweat it."

"Hmm, yes, well, believe me, I'd be delighted if I could avoid a repeat performance! As for Halloween, I'd love to, Terrence!"

"Fantastic! In that case, I'll let you get back to work. And thanks, Charlie. For your work and for… everything."

I stare at him, puzzled by his final words, but before I can ask him what he means, he waves me off, and I obediently head for the bar.

The pub is quiet this evening, and the atmosphere is one of relaxed camaraderie. Sam, afraid of Matt's wrath, makes me swear I won't tell anyone he almost saw me in my underwear. Lucas is clowning around, shoving slices of lemon into his mouth, while Chris and Tommy practice some new moves with their cocktail shakers. Fun and frolic in the pub!

Since it's so quiet, I take it easy and sit at the bar. Lucas leans in and nonchalantly points a finger at me. "You, girl, are magic!"

What's wrong with everyone tonight? Have they all been watching too much *Lord of the Rings* or something? "What are you talking about, Lucas?"

"You know, before you got here, Matt was so bad-tempered."

"Matt? Bad-tempered? Are we talking about the same guy?"

"I swear, Charlotte, since you started, he hasn't flown off the handle once.

"It's kind of hard for me to imagine…"

Sam comes over and joins the conversation. "Why do you think I asked you not to say anything about this morning? Sometimes Matt is… a handful."

"What's he talking about?" Chris asks.

"Back to work!" Sam retorts. "Mind your own business!"

"Hold on guys, are you serious?"

They nod in perfect unison, but I'm still skeptical. Maybe there have been some misunderstandings or something. Tommy intervenes now, in an attempt to sooth away some of the anxiety that their remarks have triggered. "Matt isn't bad-tempered; he's hot-headed, and he takes failure to heart. It's not the same thing. So yes, when he's stressed, he can be 'hard to handle,' but that doesn't detract from any of his great qualities. Charlie, I need to place an order tomorrow, so the stock in the cellar needs checking. Since it's slow right now, do you think you could handle it?"

"Sure, no problem, Tommy."

"Great. Lucas, can you show her the cellar and the inventory sheet?"

"Sure!"

We go downstairs to the basement and arrive in a vast room, filled with all kinds of barrels and bottles. He hands me the book of inventory sheets and a pen, and shows me how the stored bottles are categorized.

"There, young Padawan, this universe is in your hands!" Lucas says with a smile.

"Oh, you're a *Star Wars* fan too?"

"I'm way more than a fan: I don't know how many times I've watched the entire saga! George Lucas is a genius!"

"Yeah, you're right! He's given us a dark but spectacular universe!"

"Totally! We should watch all the movies together sometime! Who's your favorite character?"

Giggling wildly, I shake my hair in front of my face, and start making the trademark bizarre sounds of my beloved Chewbacca: the legendary Wookie warrior and copilot of the *Millennium Falcon*. We are soon in stitches, tears running down our faces at my rather approximate impression. Footsteps on the stairs warn us that someone is coming, and we are trying helplessly to plaster serious expressions on our faces, when Matt appears through the door.

"I'm off. Will you be okay?" Lucas asks kindly.

I'm about to open my mouth to answer him, but Matt speaks first. "It's fine! I think she can manage perfectly well BY HERSELF! There's plenty to do upstairs—a group has just arrived. Don't you think you should get back to work?"

Lucas looks at me wide-eyed and makes a face, then sidles out of the room quickly. I watch Matt as he walks towards me, noting the tension in his jaw. He wraps his arms around me, kisses me on the forehead, and holds me against him for several minutes. I let myself savor his powerful embrace. "Are you okay, Matt?"

"I am now, yes."

He uses a finger to lift my chin and kisses me softly. He looks tense and worried. He's standing right here with me, but his mind is clearly elsewhere. "Are you sure you're okay? You were a little curt with Lucas…"

"He'll get over it! I'm tired; I've had an awful day."

"You should go home and get some rest, I have to check the stock for tomorrow's order. I don't know how long I'll be."

"No! I'll stay here with you. I need to be with you. I'll help."

I'm moved by his words—and his expression: he looks like a troubled child, lost between pain and uncertainty. Despite his icy tone with Lucas, his offer warms my heart, and I forgive him for being irritable. "Are you sure? You—"

"Come on, let's start with the beer."

An hour later, we finish counting the last bottles of wine. He grabs one, and looks at me intently. "Do you like Pic Saint-Loup?"

"To be honest, I don't really know much about wine. I don't drink it often, and when I do it's white and sweet!"

"You have to taste this—it's a *Domaine de l'Hortus*. I think you'll like it!"

He grabs two glasses from a box, opens the bottle, and pours us each some wine. Then he sits on the floor with his back against the wall and invites me to sit between his legs. Pressed together, we taste this wine, savoring its notes of blackberry and vanilla. "Mmmm… It's really delicious, Matt."

"Do you know the legend of the Hortus Mountain and the Pic Saint-Loup?"

"No. Tell me!"

"They say that a long time ago, the Hortus Mountain and the Pic Saint-Loup formed a single peak. Nearby, a young shepherd fell madly in love with a young shepherdess. Under the full moon, they pledged their love: from then on, they would be inseparable. One day, their peaceful union was disrupted when a rich old merchant passing through the region fell for the young shepherdess and offered her parents gold for her hand in marriage. They accepted… Luckily, the young beauty heard about the deal, and the lovers decided to run away together. They fled, running straight ahead until they found their path blocked by a towering mountain. The merchant and his dogs were already hot on their trail. Trapped by the natural wall, not knowing what to do, they begged the gods to help them. Not far away, a giant heard their pleas, and ran to their aid. Moved by their tears, the giant struck the mountain with his fist, splitting it in two thus creating a passage through which the lovers could escape. Then the giant caught the merchant and imprisoned him in a cave. There, he began to sob, and his tears became a stream, whose waters still run to this day."

As I listen to Matt telling me this legend, I feel him start to relax behind me. I'm delighted that his irritability has dissipated. "Wonderful. But how do you know that? I'm from that region, and even I didn't know about it."

"When I arrived in France, I wanted to find out more about the region. I did a lot of reading and traveled around the area. I needed to put down new roots. Come on, we should probably get back."

When we get back upstairs to the bar, the guys are closing up, and we help them get everything ready for the next day. After we lock up, Matt takes me home. Both of us choose to be sensible and get a good night's sleep.

Shortly afterwards, I finally slide into bed, and hear my phone beep with a text.
[Good night,
dream of me as I dream of you,
sweet kisses… Chewie!
From your Valiant JEDI]

Realizing that he must have witnessed my outrageous

Chewbacca imitation, I get an attack of the giggles, and text him back.

> [Good night, Skywalker.
> Sweet dreams.
> Beware of the dark side!
> Long, sweet kisses,
> From a tired Chewie]

13. WTF…?

The sound of the rain beating down on the window panes wakes me up around 9:30. The gray sky is heavy with menacing, black clouds. Reluctantly, I drag myself out of bed, grab my phone, and go into the kitchen to fix myself an enormous cup of coffee.

"Hi, ya!" Chloé chirps, emerging from the bathroom.

She sits down at the table with me, pouring herself a cup of coffee on the way.

"You're glowing, Charlie! Did you see Matt last night?"

"Yeah, he arrived late and helped me do the inventory in the cellar."

"The inventory?" she asks suspiciously.

"Yes, the order has to go in today."

"And did the… inventory go well? Sounds pretty intimate…"

"Is that all you ever think about?!"

I smile at her silliness, shaking my head. "Nothing happened last night. It would have been tricky, anyway, given the mood he was in."

"Why?"

"Oh, he had a rough day—I've got no idea why—but when he arrived, he caught me in the cellar with Lucas who was showing me how to check the stock. We were laughing, and Matt was quite sharp with Lucas. I mean, he kind of… snapped at him and sent him out. He was really on edge…"

"But was he uptight with you?"

"Oh no! He helped me, gave me some wine to taste, and told me a fabulous legend. It was… perfect."

"Wow, everything seems to be going swimmingly between you two!"

"Yeah, but the guys told me some weird things about Matt. They said he can be kind of moody and difficult. Terrence said something strange to me too. He thanked me for my work and… 'everything.' I've got no idea what he meant, so now there are lots of questions going round in my head."

"Don't overthink it! As long as he's not hurting you and he respects you, he has my full support. Do you know how much you've changed since he came into your life, Charlie? Look at you: you're smiling again! I even heard you singing the other day. You haven't done that in ages. Live a little, Charlie! Enjoy the moment!"

It's true! Chloé is only confirming what I, myself, have been thinking. I feel alive! And every moment I spend with Matt strengthens this feeling deep inside me.

Later in the morning, he sends me a text.
[Got to go on a trip,
I'll call you as soon as I can. xxx]

My mood sinks and I suddenly feel as glum as the stormy sky. Still, I try not to let my dark thoughts get the better of me. I decide to spend my free time painting, and get out a blank canvas. I need to paint to let off some this tension.

◎ ◎ ◎

Two days go by without news from Matt. I force myself not to contact him—I don't want to disturb him at work. Anyway, I'd hate for him to think I'm desperate. At the pub, the guys try their hardest to put a smile back on my face, but his absence is bringing me down. I miss him, dammit! It's only been two days, and I'm trailing around miserably. It's pathetic! I don't know how, but he's carefully brought down my barriers and worked his way into my heart. Behind the sexy man on stage who makes hordes of women scream every weekend, there is an intelligent, gentle, passionate, and… damaged man. I'm sure of it. I can see it in the shadow that sometimes lurks in his eyes. It slips past furtively, taking him far away. That's what I saw in the cellar. What he's hiding.

◎ ◎ ◎

On Thursday morning, the phone wakes me up. Seeing his name on the screen, I'm quick to answer.

"It's me!"

"Matt! Is everything okay? I was worried!"

"I'm fine. I just can't wait to get home. I should be there tomorrow morning. I miss you, kitten!"

"I miss you too, Matt."

"Are we spending the weekend together?"

"I'd love that! Yes!"

"Promise?"

"Promise!"

I hang up, my heart swollen with joy at the idea of seeing him the next day! My good mood comes rushing back, and I decide put on some pop music and do some chores around the apartment. Chloé catches me in the act and joins me, grinding her hips like a rock star with a broom.

◎ ◎ ◎

Towards the end of the night at the pub, the boys start pestering me, wanting to know what costume I'll be wearing for Halloween.

They all have different ideas, each one crazier than the last!

"A cat?"

"A vampire?"

"A mummy?"

"Yoda in a tutu?"

"Bilbo the Hobbit?"

"Go on, tell us!"

"Stop bothering her, guys," Chris intervenes with a laugh. "Come on, let's taste our new creation: the 'Passion Valkyrie!' In honor of Charlie! To celebrate her joining the team!"

"To Charlie!" everyone choruses, raising their glasses.

The pub door opens, to reveal Matt standing in the doorway, with dark circles under his eyes. He wasn't supposed to be arriving until tomorrow morning! The tension in his muscles is palpable. He slinks towards us slowly, and something in his attitude terrifies me. It's as if an ominous anger has possessed him. When he reaches us, I'm expecting a kiss, or at least a "hello," but it never comes.

"I see you're having fun with your friends," he says coldly. "I hope I'm not disturbing you? Aren't you all supposed to be working?"

Chris chimes in immediately, trying to lighten the suddenly heavy atmosphere. "Come on, Matt, we're just taking a break to try a new cocktail dedicated to Charlie! Here, try one!"

Matt reaches out and takes the glass. He scrutinizes it, frowns, then lashes out aggressively.

"Dedicated to Charlie? Who are you to dedicate anything to her?"

He turns to me, the look in his eyes cold enough to freeze sunshine. "I see you found yourself some company, a whole fan club, in fact! It seems the time didn't go as slowly for you as it did for me!"

Then, in a blind rage, he hurls his glass against the wall. Terrence comes rushing out of his office. "Matt!" he shouts at him in a stern, forceful voice.

Glued to my bar stool in fear, I don't move. I hardly dare breathe. The lump in my throat is so big it hurts, and I can barely hold back the tears. I watch Matt follow Terrence into the office without a word. With a trembling hand, I push my glass away, staring at the floor, and get off my seat. Sam puts a hand on my shoulder, giving it a gentle squeeze.

"Don't worry about it, Charlie, it won't last. He has a short fuse, but he never stays angry for long. It'll be fine…"

Clenching my jaw, I can feel the tears gathering on my eyelashes. "It might be fine for him, but not for me," I quietly say. "My shift is over. I'm outta here."

Lucas grabs his keys and jacket, and tells me that he'll give me a ride. I pick up my bag, and we leave the pub before Matt returns.

Lucas climbs onto his motorcycle and hands me a helmet. I climb on behind him and put it on. As we set off, Matt runs out. "Charlie!" he hollers.

Too late.

Lucas accelerates and we speed off down the street. Blinded by my tears, I can't even make out the road in front of me. Nausea washes over me, and I cling tighter to Lucas, feeling dizzy. We haven't even been riding five minutes when I tap him on the back and gesture for him to pull over. He stops and I run off to puke in a ditch.

When I have completely emptied my stomach, I go back to him. He hands me a tissue and looks at me with concern in his eyes. "Are you gonna be okay, Charlie?"

Suddenly, I can't hold back the tears anymore. Lucas leaps over and wraps his arms around me. I cry and cry and cry. He rocks me gently, trying to soothe me.

"It's okay, Charlie. Shh… Shall we take a walk? Or would you rather go home? It's your call."

"I… I'm scared he'll come to my place. I don't feel ready to face him yet. Take me for a ride on your bike…"

"At your service!"

We get back on the bike and ride for almost half an hour before he slows down and pulls over to a patch of grass. We don't say anything. We just lie down on the grass, side by side.

"Do you want to talk, Charlie?"

"Don't tell me you want to listen to me whining and sniveling, Lucas. Unless you're some kind of masochist!"

"Maybe we could talk about your reaction to his anger, for example. About how terrified you were. I'm not blind, Charlie. Something pretty ugly has happened to you, and you're carrying it around."

"Great! Am I really that transparent?"

"No… but it's obvious to someone who's experienced it."

I stare at him, unable to believe what I'm hearing. "You…"

"No, not me. My sister. She got involved with a bastard who gave her a really hard time, and just now, I saw the same demons in your eyes. He'd never hurt you, Charlie. He's not like that. He's a good guy, I promise, but he has his own demons."

"What do you mean?"

"I mean that all of us react differently to the damages that life inflicts upon us. Matt explodes easily, but he calms down quickly. He doesn't talk about his feelings much; he expresses himself through his music and his actions instead. He's a reserved guy, but a good one. And… you're good for him, Charlie."

"That's not the impression I got this evening. He was

absolutely furious when he looked at me. And it hurt! There was no reason for him to react the way he did. We weren't doing anything wrong..."

"His bad mood wasn't directed at you, and what you thought was anger was merely jealousy. Matt has become really attached to you. Let things blow over; tomorrow is another day."

"Wow, where did all this wisdom come from?"

He bursts out laughing and runs a hand through his hair with a smile.

"Two years of psychology in college!"

"You should open a clinic, you'd be rich!"

Laughing again, he asks me if I'm feeling better and if I am ready to go home.

I nod, and we get back on his bike. "Thanks, Lucas."

"Any time, Charlie. That'll be a hundred and fifty euros!"

He winks and chuckles at his joke.

He drops me off, gives me a peck on the cheek, and orders me to go and get some sleep.

It's already past 2:30 in the morning. I sneak in, but Chloé is sitting there, waiting for me with a cup of coffee in her hand. "You're not in bed?"

"Spit it out! What happened? Boom Boom woke me up, making one hell of a racket. He was completely out of sorts. Actually, come to think of it, his nickname suits him perfectly. I thought he was going to break the door down. Is your cell phone not working again?"

The tears spring to my eyes again, and sobs shake my body as I collapse onto the chair. Chloé dashes over to me and squeezes me hard.

I'm exhausted by this evening, exhausted by everything I've been through these past 48 hours.

I blurt out the details of my night: Matt's tantrum, my fear, what Lucas said, what the others said, my decision not to come home straight away, my doubts and my fears. Everything comes pouring out... I tell her about his radical change in behavior this evening, how angry I am at him, at those words he so coldly threw in my face.

He hurt me! Deeply and deliberately!

Chloé is flabbergasted, and she admits she is just as confused as I am.

"One thing's for sure, Charlie: if he didn't have feelings for you, he wouldn't have shown up here with his eyes all red. But that's no excuse for his behavior! Do you want me to castrate him?"

"I'm so glad I've got you... You always make me smile, even when everything turns to shit. I don't know what to do. It's probably best I put an end to this relationship now. There is no future in it anyway. As soon as he finds out, he'll obviously want to move on. I..."

"Don't go trying to predict the future, sweetie. You can't be sure of anything! Hear him out first. If you don't like what he has to say, you have my permission to bite! Come on, let's go to bed. You're exhausted."

14. Got my Goat

I toss and turn all night long, my nightmares a cocktail of past and present, and when my alarm rings, I am actually relieved. My mind still foggy with sleep, I see Chloé poke her head in the door and shoulder her way into the room, carrying a tray loaded with food.

"Hey… how are you feeling this morning?"

"You mean aside from the crushing disappointment and frustration? I'm furious, Chloé!"

"Oh, I know, sweetie, that's why I brought you this!"

"Did you hold up the grocery store?"

"Ha ha, very funny. No, we're having breakfast in bed!"

"Thanks. You're an angel."

I lower my gaze, thoughts of Matt invading my brain.

"Hey, misery guts! What's on your mind?"

"Matt. I need a day to recover. I don't really want him showing up here unannounced."

"That won't be happening. I had him on the phone at six this morning."

"6 AM?"

"Yeah. I told him to give you some space today. Anyway, we're spending the day at Emily's. She's expecting us at ten."

"You're the best!"

"Yeah, I know. I am pretty good at this sort of thing!"

◎ ◎ ◎

When I walk into the Green Country that evening, my stomach is churning painfully. I'm feeling panicky, but a quick scan of the room reassures me that he's not around yet. The boys try to comfort me with soothing words, which help briefly.

I throw myself into my work, trying not to think too much in case I lose my grip. Twenty minutes later, I hear music coming from the stage, and I know he's there. I don't even turn around, but I can feel the weight of his gaze on the back of my neck.

I try to stay dignified, battling to maintain control over my brain and body, and I focus on clearing the table. I have almost finished when I feel his hand on my arm.

"Can we talk?"

I pull away violently, as if his hand had burned me.

"Don't touch me! Leave me alone and let me work."

He pulls the tray from my hands and places it on the table, leaving no room for argument. "We have to talk!"

"Well, I think you've said too much already! LEAVE ME ALONE!"

In an instant, he has lifted me up and is carrying me on his shoulder.

"For fuck's sake, Matt! Put me down, right now!"

Ignoring my protests, he strides across the room and takes me into the kitchen, where he puts me down.

"Son of a bitch! Who do you think you are? I work here. The place is packed with people—you have no right to do this!"

"I asked you nicely."

"So? That doesn't mean I have to listen. Asking nicely today doesn't change how you behaved yesterday! You can't just treat me any which way! I'm angry, and I have every reason to be! You were way out of line, for no reason at all."

"I'm sorry, I…"

"You're sorry? Hell, Matt. Saying you're sorry is too easy, don't you think?"

"Dammit, I'm trying to apologize! Won't you at least hear me out? I had a really shit day yesterday… worse than shit. Two nights without sleep! I was exhausted, I'd had enough, and—"

"Oh…! And that means you don't have to behave like a civilized human being, does it? I mean, what the fuck was that, anyway? Does that mean that every time things aren't going well, you're going to act like a pig? Am I meant to carry on a relationship with Dr. Jekyll and Mr. Hyde? Is that what you're saying? Well, I think I'll pass, thanks. As you know, I've already had my fair share of degenerates! I refuse to take on any more. There's no way in hell."

I turn my back on him and burst into tears. It's all too much for my nerves to take. He comes over and wraps his arms around me. I push him away and try to wrestle my way free, but he just tightens his grip, kissing me on top of my head.

"Don't compare me to that nameless brute, please! I will never hurt you! Just give me a chance to prove myself. I'm not a monster. I was just so desperate to see you again. And yesterday, when I arrived and saw you surrounded by all the guys, I felt so… unworthy of you, like you deserve so much better."

"What are you trying to say?"

"I've got my own baggage. My parents, the horrors of the army… certain memories that are hard to deal with."

I turn around and look at him. There are shadows dancing in his eyes, darkening them, and my heart wrenches. He's starting to open up. "We all have our demons, Matt," I say gently, "but we can't take them out on the whole world and attack the people close to us every time we are having a bad day. And I never want to hear you say you're unworthy of me, ever again. Dammit! You're the best thing that's happened to me these last few years."

He cups my face in his hands, locks his gaze onto mine and kisses me fervently. Kissing him back, I cling to him, abandoning myself to his embrace, because right now, all I want to do is chase away our demons. Even if only for a moment.

"So, am I forgiven, kitten?"

"You'll need to prove yourself."

After a brief pause, I tell him we should be getting back to work, even though I would love to have a bit longer in the kitchen alone with him. "I think we've been trying the boss's patience a bit too often recently, Matt."

"The boss is very understanding, but you're right, we should get back."

"How do you think he'll react to that little display we put on just now? We made quite a scene…"

"Only because you're as stubborn as a mule!"

"Only because you're as obstinate as a goat!"

He bursts out laughing. "We could open a zoo! To be honest," he adds. "I think he'll be glad you barked at me and put me in my place. He thinks very highly of you, especially the Valkyrie in you. Don't worry. Come on, let's go…"

As we walk through the door, he smacks my butt, winks, and gives me a winning smile. He heads towards the stage, and I go to find Lucas, who gives me a knowing look. "So did you guys sign a peace treaty?"

"You could say that, yes…"

"Nice work, champ!"

The crowd begins to gather, and we are soon engulfed in a wave of rhythmic madness. The group this evening is playing *really* hard rock, and the atmosphere is pulsing. Terrence, who until now was probably in his office, is stationed in a corner, carefully watching the crowd. He catches my eye and walks towards me, looking relaxed. "Terrence, I—"

He slips an arm around my shoulder and nods towards Matt, who is chatting with one of the musicians. "If it happens again," he says into my ear, "If Matt flies off the handle, you have my permission to slap him! In fact, you have my blessing."

A murmur spreads across the room when Matt appears on stage and begins addressing the crowd. "I hope you're all having a good time tonight. I just wanted to say a few words. I'm not really into giving speeches, but sometimes, people don't say what they feel often enough… When you're surrounded by friends who support you, who put up with your mood swings, who are patient and loyal, it's important to thank them. So this evening, I'd like to thank the team who serve you here every night. Thanks, guys! I'd also like to introduce our new recruit, who I'm sure most of you've already met. I'm talking about Charlotte, who has been a huge hit with the entire team from the get-go!"

The rest of the team, all gathered at my side, start whistling, and grab my hands, lifting them into the air triumphantly.

"Here's to Charlie!" Sam cries.

"That's it, Charlie, you're more than my champion now: you're my idol!" Lucas tells me proudly.

As the crowd applauds, Matt continues his speech. "To

celebrate, we're going to jam with the band here this evening, the Squadmonsters. We're going to cover a rock classic: Led Zeppelin's 'Whole Lotta Love!'"

The room goes wild and I find myself dragged onto the dance floor by the happy little gang. The guys take turns to dancing with me, spinning around and laughing. Even Terrence lets go and does a few dance steps. Our zest for life comes rushing back, pushing away yesterday's stress.

When the song ends, Matt whispers a few words in the ear of the lead singer, who addresses the crowd, "Yeah! It's time for a cult classic—this one's dedicated to someone special…"

Matt climbs down from the stage, his eyes fixed on me, and makes his way through the crowd to join me. I'd know this song anywhere! "Broken" by Seether: the music from *The Crow*.

The first movie we watched together. My movie. This gesture from Matt goes straight to my heart. Of the thousands of songs he could have chosen, he picked this one. He holds out his hand, smiling playfully, and drags me out onto the dance floor, where he takes me in his arms. We start swaying to the soulful notes. With his hand gently moving on the hollow of my back, our bodies fit together perfectly, sensually. He sings in my ear, letting his breath caress my neck. I think back to what Lucas said: Matt expresses himself through the lyrics. Like a hidden confession. In fact, he's not singing, he's talking to me, communicating in his own way—the subtlest way possible.

> *I wanted you to know I love the way you laugh*
> *I wanna hold you high and steal your pain away*
>
> …
>
> *I wanna hold you high and steal your pain*
> *'Cause I'm broken when I'm lonesome*
> *And I don't feel right when you're gone away*
> *You're gone away*
>
> …
>
> *The worst is over now and we can breathe again*

When the song is over, he lifts my chin and drops the softest of kisses on my lips. Then he lets me get back to work. I watch him weave back through the crowd, his warmth and scent still lingering on my skin.

There are moments in life, however fleeting, which take on a rare and precious quality, because of their emotional intensity, because they are sincere and deeply redeeming. This feels like one of those moments…

I go about my work in an almost blissful state, simply smiling at the jokes the guys make for the rest of the evening.

Everything is back to normal: laughter, good vibes, camaraderie… I love this job! And I love the people I work with. I keep catching Matt checking me out. It's like he doesn't want to break the link that held us together earlier. He's watching me from a distance, observing me, devouring me with his eyes. His gaze seems to strip me bare, burning right through my little white dress. He's watching my reaction. I feel enveloped in his aura, like I am nestled in a protective, reassuring cocoon.

At around 2 o'clock, the final customers leave the pub and we clean up the last traces of the evening. Just as we are getting ready to leave for the night, turning off the lights and letting the darkness take over, Matt catches my hand and squeezes it tightly.

"You go on ahead, guys, I'll close up…"

15. Taste of Ecstasy

I look at him with questioning eyes. He flicks the latch on the door, so we won't be interrupted, and we find ourselves ensconced in intimacy.

"I don't want this night to end…"

He pulls a remote control out of the back pocket of his jeans, and the music rises up again, enchanting and overwhelming. The Scorpions: "Always Somewhere." The lyrics are beautiful, a declaration in themselves.

A night without you seems like a lost dream
Love I can't tell you how I feel
Always somewhere
Miss you where I've been
I'll be back to love you again…

Matt takes me in his arms and we dance, alone, in the middle of the dance floor—the sole witnesses of our mutual desire. We don't need words. We just need to touch, breathe, and tame each other. He lifts me up with one hand under each buttock, my legs knot around his waist, and we keep dancing, tangled together as one on the dance floor. The thin straps of my dress slide slowly down my shoulders, helped along by his adventurous teeth. I clutch onto his broad shoulders as he drops a string of kisses down my neck. I tip my head back further, savoring every caress, letting myself get lost in his embrace. He keeps dancing in a sultry sway, without missing a beat. He takes his time, breaking down my resistance little by little, with exquisite slowness, lingering over every movement of his hips.

His lips stray to my mouth and he lets his tongue work its way in. He buries one hand in my hair, grabbing my neck, holding me at the mercy of his tender, passionate kiss. This is how we remain for a magical moment, savoring each other, rediscovering each other, exploring the delicious sensations that we share. Reality seems to melt away, leaving us alone with the intense beating of our hearts.

My senses are on fire, demanding more... much more... much, much more of him. I want him...

One song fades into another, Bon Jovi's "Bed of Roses" forming the background to our embrace.

I don't know if it is the deeply erotic title that does it, be we are soon sucked in completely, abandoning ourselves to each other. Matt slowly places me on the edge of a table and gently lays me down, letting his hands slip down between my breasts then slide under my dress to take off my panties. Everything that follows comes in an overpowering stream of sensations, whisking me even further from reality. My body becomes a puppet to which he holds the strings. I plunge into a sea of ecstasy, tasting alternative paradises. When Matt lets himself slip inside me, nothing else seems to matter, as we let bodies take over, filling each other greedily. Driving himself into me hard, he whisks us up in a whirlwind of carnal pleasures, leading the dance. Our bodies complete each other, pressed together in search of total harmony. His powerful thrusts, penetrating me deeper and deeper, are totally unbridled. Raw and possessive, he makes me his, letting his volcanic nature pour out. He draws on it for strength, each assault passing his power on to me. We become one body, and our orgasm erupts in unison, leaving us breathless and drunk with pleasure.

He lifts me up in his arms and takes me through a door that leads straight to his apartment. Still giddy and trembling, I snuggle into him, exhausted, and amazed that I have met this wonderful man.

◎◎◎

In the early hours of the morning, I notice that Matt is stretched out beside me, watching me in silence. The sheet draped over his waist reveals his sculpted torso. Lying on my tummy, I ogle him freely. His brazen nonchalance is there, as ever, almost as if yesterday were just a dream. But no: my entire body bears testament to it, still aching from his ardor. He plants a kiss on my shoulder and rolls onto his side.

"Good morning…"

"Good morning…"

He is nibbling his bottom lip, his eyes glued to me, a daring smile fluttering around his mouth.

"Rested?"

"A bit achy!"

"Mmmm… overindulged?"

I nod my head, grinning and blushing as I think back to last night. "Just… in a delicious daze."

He rolls over onto me, tangles his fingers in mine, rests on the pillow, and kisses the curve of my neck. With his pelvis pushed up against mine, rocking gently, I can feel him getting hard against my butt.

"You're just way too tempting. Look what you do to me."

"I don't know what you're talking about. I haven't moved an inch."

"Exactly! It's just… the way you are."

"I don't think I'm in any mood for a repeat performance right now. I'm still a bit numb, and—"

"Uh-huh, lack of endurance. That's something we can work on. It's just a question of habit. I'd feel bad if I neglected your training, kitten! But I'll let you rest for now. Until tonight that is! Come on, let's get some food."

We decide to go out to eat, so we get ready and go in search of somewhere to satisfy our morning appetites. After wandering around for half an hour, we choose an old-style brasserie.

The selection of pastries and other treats on offer here is off the charts. We take our time selecting a few, before perching ourselves on one of the long benches. This private morning moment is the perfect time for a relaxed chat about our tastes.

"So you like rock classics?"

He is looking at me intensely, smiling slightly at this allusion to our moment last night. "I like lots of things. But yeah, I'm a big fan of the great rock classics. What about you?"

"I have pretty varied tastes, as long as the music makes me feel something, or the words really mean something. There are songs I just fall in love with."

"And what's your current crush?"

"Oh, I'm test-driving a new one right now!"

"And you know what they say! There's nothing like a well-oiled machine. I like to explore everything deeply, keep things lubricated and... running smoothly."

I laugh at his rebellious expression and his words bursting with innuendo, then bite into the enormous praline brioche I have in my hands. "Oh my god, this thing is like an orgasm for the taste buds. It's exquisite! Wanna try?"

He devours me with his eyes, shamelessly, making no attempt to hide his lust. "Hell, yeah!"

He gets up, leans over the table and gives me a sensuous kiss, licking the sugar from my lips. He holds my neck gently yet possessively as he meticulously caresses me with the tip of his tongue.

When his appetite is satisfied, he gives me his now familiar expression, the one that means "I came, I saw, I conquered."

"Eat!"

Eat, eat. He really knows how to get me going... my hormones are raging! How does he always stay so cool and collected, when I'm a total mess?

He's shockingly bold and yet unbelievably sexy, and he's sitting here, opposite me. I don't know what he sees in me. I'm hardly supermodel material, I'm no good at relationships—I'm broken in that respect—and he's the total opposite. His interest in me is a mystery. Still, I'd be the first to admit that being around him is therapeutic, and I'm enjoying letting myself go little by little.

When we've finished our little feast, we decide to go for a walk. We opt for a stroll around the city's gardens, with their fountains, waterfalls, and all kinds of flowers: a wonderful place to explore.

He holds my hand tenderly as we walk, twisting his fingers through mine.

"I'm really sorry about the other night…"

"It's fine, Matt. We already talked it through. I think we've said all there is to say."

"I feel really bad about it. The last thing I want to do is hurt you!"

"Well, I guess I'd just say, try not do it again!"

"I know. I have to prove myself."

"Exactly!"

"And I've made a good start, right? Like, yesterday, when you said yes!"

"What do you mean, I said yes?"

He turns to face me, links his hands together behind my back, and gives me a devilish smile. "Yes. Yesterday, on the table, you were saying: 'yeeesss!'"

"Oh! You… you…"

"… great, stunning, and amazing lover?"

"… great arrogant goat would be more like it!"

Unable to stop laughing, we sit down underneath a willow tree, similar to the one under which we shared our first special moment together. The firefly tree. He tips me back into his arms and looks at me intently.

"How do you see yourself in the future?"

"I have a hard time thinking about the future. Life is too unpredictable. It's waiting around the corner, ready to stomp all over you. I'd rather avoid disappointment as much as possible."

"But you've got to dream!"

"I've stopped dreaming, Matt."

He gently strokes my hair, twirling a lock of it around his finger. "I have to tell you something," he says, his voice husky.

His phone suddenly rings, interrupting him. He shakes his head, looking deeply annoyed, but answers anyway. "Hello? Yes… No… No… Yes, I'm coming."

He hangs up, frustrated, and looks at me in dismay.

"I've got to go, urgent business to deal with. I'm sorry. Don't be mad."

"You look worried, is everything okay?"

"I don't know. I'll know later. I've got to go. Shall I drive you home?"

"No, it's okay, I'll walk."

He gives me a tight squeeze, then walks off quickly. I pick up my bag and stroll home along the boulevards. Lost in my thoughts, I don't even notice the drops of rain starting to fall. Suddenly, it hits me: it's Saturday. Another call, another hasty departure. Where on earth does he go?

When I get back to the apartment, I head directly for my bedroom. My head aches from all the thoughts jostling around in my mind. He was going to say something earlier, just before his phone rang. Too many questions, not enough answers. I spend a good part of the day wallowing in worry, with fear and uncertainty fighting for space in my brain. I hope this return will be less disturbing than the last one. I couldn't deal with a repeat. And there's no way I could bear a man unleashing his hatred upon me again.

In my mind, I picture it all again: the gun pointed at me, his finger on the trigger... Then his hands on my neck, squeezing harder and harder... His sick little game of Russian roulette, with every pull of the trigger making me scream with fear. Once that terror gets inside you, it will always be there. Then the cries, the threats, the insults. The broken objects all around me. Now I'm broken too. A direct consequence of an emotional shock that was too brutal to handle, crushing all my hopes and dreams...

These dark thoughts go around and around in my head until the tears come streaming down my face. I don't even try to hold them back. The sound of the front door opening startles me, and I quickly brush the tears away.

When Chloé comes in, she can sense the suffering that is eating away at me. She comes over and sits by my side. I bury my face in her shoulder, and she rocks me gently. "It's going to be okay, Charlie. Did something happen?"

"No, we were together and he got another phone call. He went off to deal with something. His boss must be a real asshole to call him during the weekend and expect him to come running like that. But after what happened last time, all my fears bubbled back up and..."

"It'll be different this time. And if it's not, he'll have to answer to me! Don't spend time and energy worrying about something that might not happen. Come on, let's fix ourselves a little snack."

I'm dubious. I don't know what to think any more. Despite Chloé's attempts to reassure me, I can't help but expect the worst.

16. Jackal Boys

It's 7:15 in the evening when my phone rings. It's Lucas, wanting to talk to Matt urgently. Terrence has been in a car accident: nothing serious, but they're going to keep him under observation until tomorrow. "Okay, but why is it so important to let Matt know? He'll find out when he gets back. If it's not serious, then why worry him?"

"Uh... Because... He's the one who has the keys to the pub, and we can't open up without him."

I tell him Matt isn't with me, because he had to leave for some professional emergency, but that I'll try to contact him. We agree to keep each other posted, and I hang up. I pick up my phone and try to call Matt, but it goes straight to voicemail, so I leave a message. I turn to Chloé, feelings of doubt creeping into my mind. "His phone is off. It goes straight to voicemail."

"Or maybe he has no signal, Charlotte! Give it a minute and try again!"

At around 8, I still can't get hold of him, so I send two texts, five minutes apart. "Where is he, dammit? In a black hole or something?"

At 8:30, my phone rings, and I am relieved to see Matt's name on the screen.

"Sorry, I just got your messages. Terrence called too, he's fine. I'll be there to open the pub. Could you call Lucas for me?"

"Sure, I'm on it."

"Hey, kitten!"

"Yes?"

"Ready to train again this evening? Bring some spare clothes. You won't be going home!"

I hang up, smiling, and call Lucas.

When I get to the pub, Chris, Sam, and Tommy are there, but I don't see Matt or Lucas. I put my things down and go over to say hello. "Have Matt and Lucas deserted us?"

"Don't worry, they're on their way!" Tommy answers.

I start work. It's pretty quiet, and the customers trickle in slowly.

I'm serving a table of four when I hear angry shouts coming from the office. "You'd better tell her quickly, dammit! I refuse to go on like this, Matt. Do you hear me?"

Lucas storms out in a huff, which startles me. He glances over, then lowers his eyes, and slinks behind the bar. I stay where I am, perfectly still, not knowing what to do. In the end, I decide to play it off as if nothing had happened. If they have scores to settle, I'd rather not get involved.

When I go behind the bar, Lucas comes over to me and gives me a kiss on my temple. "Everything okay, Lucas?"

"Yeah, fine, Charlie, just a… disagreement. Not to worry!"

Just then, Matt comes out of the office. They stare each other up and down. I don't know what's going on between those two, but the animosity in the air is unmistakable.

Chris intervenes, taking Lucas to one side, and Matt comes over to me. He takes me by the hand and leads me into the kitchen. This is starting to become a habit. Once we are alone, he pins me against the wall, holding my hands over my head, and kisses me passionately. Gradually, I feel his body relax, as if our kiss is erasing his tension. He slides a leg between my thighs, forcing them open, and pushes his hips against mine, moving very suggestively.

"God, I want you!" He breathes into my lips.

Panting in the heat of his desire, I feel a stirring between my legs, intimate sparks crackling. He drives me totally wild. His scent envelops me, making me dizzy. It's insane how much he turns me on. I try to curb my desire, and lift my gaze to his face. His expression is intense as he battles to keep his self-control. "We're at work, Matt."

"I know, but I needed to feel you against me."

"This isn't reasonable."

"I don't want to be reasonable."

"Well, you'll have to be. I have to get back to work. Just because the boss isn't here doesn't mean we can act like horny teenagers. Terrence is counting on us. We can't go being all irresponsible."

"Alright, if the boss is counting on us! Just you wait until later, though…"

He pulls away and we go back to work.

At around 10:30, Emily and Chloé show up. They greet me warmly, then go and look for a free table. Matt will be on soon, and the women are already gathering around the stage. I'm not sure if I can get used to this…

The air turns electric as our typical Saturday evening crowd starts to swell.

Sam asks me if I'm coping, and I nod.

"You're awesome, Charlie!" He says with a smile.

As soon as Matt takes possession of the stage, our job suddenly gets a lot harder. Carrying the trays becomes almost impossible, but we are graceful enough to avoid disaster. Luckily, I had the good sense to wear jeans, which makes it much easier to move around the room. I have completed my outfit with a floaty, turquoise top and gray thigh-high boots. I feel relaxed and comfortable, despite the chaos on the dance floor.

A song I don't yet know starts: "Kick the Dust Up."

The bass and rhythm of this typically country tune are exhilarating. Everyone stampedes onto the dance floor. Suddenly, over the noise, I hear Chris and Sam shouting at me. Both are standing on the bar, calling to me to join them. I shake my head, laughing. No way! Never in a million years! But they won't take no for an answer: Tommy and Lucas pull me over to the bar and lift me onto it. Then they climb up there with me.

I find myself in the middle, and it's not long before I am line dancing with them. I'm dying with shame and laughter, but I follow their steps, giving in to the madness. It's like being in a remake of the *Coyote Ugly*. We could call our new movie the *Jackal Ugly*. I soon get into it, and all five of us are showing off our moves, as Chloé and Emily shriek with laughter, not missing a moment of the action. I can't tell what Matt is enjoying more: singing or watching us clown around on top of the bar. When one of the guys propped up against the bar tries to touch me, Lucas deliberately steps on his fingers, crushing them mercilessly. The poor guy doesn't push it, and backs off. Lucas looks at Matt, who thanks him with a quick nod of his head. He nods back. Their friendship is baffling: loyal but explosive...

As soon as the song is over, the boys help me down off the bar, and after a group hug, we get back to work. Around an hour later, I take a break and sit down with the girls at their table. Sam is being pretty obvious, lurking around us. Then, when he comes over to serve us our drinks, he proudly announces that they are on the house! We thank him, and he suddenly dives in to give Chloé a kiss on the neck. She doesn't really resist. Emily and I share a knowing look, and clink our glasses together merrily. Matt announces another new song. I look up and realize that it is the composition that got him out of bed last weekend.

"Great, a new one. Do you know it, Charlotte?"

"I'm not sure. It sounds a bit like 'Ode to a G-String!'"

Between two bursts of laughter, I relate, in a hushed voice, the details of finding him that morning with my panties in the pocket of his jeans, writing a song. We are all still giggling when Matt reveals the title: "I Don't Want This Night to End."

I am speechless, as memories of his deep tenderness that night resurface. Emily and Chloé watch me, their faces softening. As Matt sings the first words of the song, I look down and blush. He doesn't take his eyes off me for a second.

Darling, I know that I don't know you.
But your eyes are so pretty, your eyes are so blue.
They draw me in like your skin beneath the moon.
I'm so happy you trust me, casting light upon this gloom.

...

You look so sexy.
And I don't know what road we're on.

...

Darling all I know is that I don't want this night to end.

...

I'd do anything for your smile,
To land upon my lips awhile,
To drown me in your kiss a while longer.
Darling all I know is that I don't want this night to end.

I am nibbling my bottom lip, my heart swollen from this declaration. I feel so emotional and overwhelmed that I can't move. I don't know what to do. I feel like I'm being watched... and with good reason: the guys are standing in a little cluster, staring at me with knowing smiles.

"You're done for, babe. If that's not an admission of love, I'll get a cock transplanted onto my forehead!" Chloé says, sure of herself.

"There's no doubt about it, Charlotte. I'm with Chloé on this one. This is way more than just lust!" Emily adds.

"I…"

"No point intellectualizing what you feel. Just let it happen, Charlotte."

"Right, I'm going back to work!"

The night is nearly over, and I get moving, clearing the remaining tables. The girls are still there, chatting with Chris and Sam at the bar, while Tommy and Lucas put away the last bottles. Matt joins me, placing one hand on my back and kissing me softly on the forehead. "Come on, we're done for the evening, let's go and join the others."

We sit down with them and Tommy pours us one, last drink. Then suddenly, Chris pulls a flier out of his pocket.

"Hey, would you be into going to the carnival together tomorrow?"

Matt looks at me to see what I think, and I grin like a little kid, nodding my head vigorously. Everyone seems delighted by the idea, and we agree to meet at ten outside the pub.

Matt circles a possessive arm around my waist, pulls me to him and gets up from his bar stool, leading me towards the door to his apartment.

"On that note, we're out of here! Tommy, can you close up?"

"No problem! See you two tomorrow!"

Without a word, we slip into his apartment and head for the living room. I drop my bag by the sofa, and I am pulling off my thigh-high boots when I feel him just behind me. He spins me around to face him. His gaze is glued to me, his eyes gray and unmoving, filled with questions. He looks like there's a war waging inside his head, like he is torn. He half opens his lips, but no words come out. Just a long sigh, with a minty aroma. His arms sweep me off the ground, and still without a word, he carries me to his bedroom. He gently puts me down, sits on the armchair with his thighs parted, and pulls me to him by the edge of my top. His hands are exploring underneath the fabric, stroking my stomach, every movement making me quiver.

"Take your top off…"

His warm, velvety voice is hypnotic, and I obey, pulling my top over my head and letting it drop to my feet.

He stays there, immobile, his eyes exploring my body until they find my breasts.

"Take this off too," he says, pointing to my bra.

I remove my last barrier, offering the swell of my breasts for him to admire. He moves forward, kisses my stomach just beneath my navel, and slips his index finger into my jeans, his thumb pushing from the outside to undo the buttons. One by one, he pops them open, then he pulls my jeans down and helps me out of them.

I see his eyes glisten with surprise as he discovers my white lace panties, held up by a dainty pink ribbon on each side. Slowly, he caresses the elastic trim, tracing the curve of my buttocks. Then, he pulls on each bow, letting the scrap of lace fall to the floor.

"Open your legs; let me look at you."

The power he exudes is slightly intimidating, yet somehow gentle. I throw self-consciousness to the wind and do as he asks. The palm of his hand caresses my inner thigh, slowly working its way upwards… He slips his hand between my legs, his thumb brushing my clitoris, indulging it with little, circular movements. I tilt my head back, letting the exquisite sensations spread through me.

"Yes, that's it. Let yourself go…"

He keeps up this delectable torture for several moments then dives into me with one of his fingers. Caressing every last intimate part, he sends a series of electric shocks throughout my body. When he pulls his finger out of me, he brings it to his lips to taste the nectar my pleasure, groaning with satisfaction. He grabs my buttocks and sits me on top of him. His lips trap mine, taking possession of them. His tongue licks the edges of my lips, playing, teasing, slipping inside to find mine, dancing around it. With one palm pinned to my back, he uses the other to tip me backwards, slowly working his mouth down between my breasts. He lingers over a nipple, pinching it with his teeth then sucking gently. Then he stands, holding me up with his arms, and lays me on the bed.

In a flash, he whips off his jeans, boxers, and T-shirt, so that his naked body towers over me. Time for a hard night's training…

17. Secret Identity

In the morning, the bed is empty. I get up, throw on the shorts and tank top I brought with me, and go into the living room in search of Matt. I find him leaning against the window, his gaze lost in the distance, with an obscure anguish visibly eating away at him. I softly walk over, troubled by the dark expression on his face.

"Morning…"

"What's going on, Matt?"

"I need to talk to you. And I don't know where to start."

I feel my stomach twist into a knot. Seeing him this serious frightens me. "Tell me, Matt…"

"Promise you'll hear me out."

"Yes, of course, just say it already! You're scaring me."

He lifts me up and places me on the windowsill, parting my knees with his hands and sliding into the gap.

"The pub, the Green Country… It belongs to me."

"What do you mean, the pub belongs to you? You mean you feel at home there?"

"No, I mean the pub belongs to me, I own the place. Terrence is the manager, I'm the owner."

I look at him, unable to believe my ears. Is this some kind of a joke?! It's got to be! I'm about to jump off my perch, but Matt takes me in his arms and lays my head against his chest. "You're joking! Tell me you're joking!"

"No, I'm serious."

"So you're my boss? YOU… ARE… MY… BOSS! SHIT! Matt!"

I try to wrestle my way out of his arms, but he only holds me tighter, refusing to let me go.

"Hear me out! Please! When we advertised the job, we were planning to hire a man. But we had to write 'waiter/waitress' to avoid discrimination issues. And you applied. When I saw you, Terrence persuaded me to hire you. It was the first time he'd suggested hiring a woman. After your interview, he told me I'd made the right choice taking you on. The next day, when we bumped into each other, when I held you in my arms for the first time, I knew I wanted more... Then everything happened so fast. And I didn't know how to tell you..."

"Maybe you should have told me before you started toying with me like some kind of puppet, and let me decide for myself!"

"I didn't want you to push me away. You were so... distant and uncompromising. Then we started getting close, and I didn't want to lose you. If I had told you from the start who I was, do you think we'd be where we are today?"

"No, no way, that's for sure! I can't sleep with my boss! You lied to me! You..."

"Yes, I lied, because I couldn't stand the thought of being without you! You've turned my brain inside-out. Can't you understand that? I've fallen in love with you... What's so bad about that? In your world, you reject people, but here, now, the two of us, it's real. I'm crazy about you, kitten! Please, this thing between us, it's precious. Don't throw it all away just because of a technicality on a piece of paper."

Dazed and confused, I struggle to take it all in. My head is overcrowded with thoughts. I'm at a loss for words.

"I'm not asking you to say the same thing back to me. I just want you to understand how I feel about you. I've already told you, I never meant to hurt you."

"I don't know, Matt."

"I know you're still on the defensive, but at least give *us* a chance. Please."

He cups my face in his hands and places his lips on mine. "Don't leave me..."

My heart breaks in half when I see his eyes mist up, a man so strong and... Dammit! I can't bear to see him suffering. "I'm not leaving you, Matt. I just need time. My heart is still... too..."

"Whatever you need, my love."

I head towards the kitchen, pressing my hand to my forehead. I can feel a migraine coming on. With the shock of this news, on the heels of the oncoming stress and fatigue, it's not surprising really. Matt comes in as I'm picking up the coffee press. He stands behind me and rests his chin on my head. His arms curl around my waist, and he pulls my body into his.

"I'm sorry."

We stand that way for some time, me seeking comfort in the arms of the man who has just confessed that he mislead me, and him refusing to let me go. After a long pause, he lifts me up and sits me on the edge of the central island. He rests his forehead against mine before he speaks. "Say something..."

"I'll be OK. I just have a killer headache."

He picks up a glass and fills it with water, opens a drawer and passes me a vial of painkillers.

"Here, take one of these, they're pretty potent."

I throw back a pill with a gulp of water and put the glass down next to me. Matt gazes at me intensely. He looks bewildered and terribly distressed. I don't know why, but I get the impression he's waiting for some kind of sign from me, some kind of reassuring gesture. Suddenly, he looks very fragile. I can't bring myself to leave him like this, so I reach out a hand, take hold of the bottom of his T-shirt, and pull him close. I wrap my arms around his waist and bury my face in his strong chest. His hand comes to the back of my head, and I hear him sigh deeply. His heartbeat, which was quick and irregular, gradually slows, and I feel the relief flooding through him.

"Do you still want to meet the others?"

"Sure. It would be nice to hang out at the carnival."

"Okay then, we should get ready, because we've only got about 20 minutes!"

"Oh shit! Umm, okay, I'll jump in the shower."

I slip off the island and speed down the hall.

"I'll jump in with you!" he calls out after me.

"Oh no you won't! If you do that, we'll never get there! So keep out!"

"But—"

"Scram!"

His face takes on the sulky expression of a little boy. "You're a mean old broad!" he says accusingly.

"Yes, and you can count your blessings, boss! You deserve much worse! How about a week of total abstinence?"

"No, surely you wouldn't?"

I take refuge in the bathroom and shut the door behind me. I'm practically doubled over in laughter at his dismay, but I'm determined to let him stew.

◎ ◎ ◎

When we catch up with the group, Chloé is already there, perched on Sam's motorbike, and the others are sitting on the ground, still looking sleepy.

"Hey, what kept you?"

"Come on, Tommy! We're not even five minutes late!"

"Yeah, but you only had to walk five yards!"

He has a point! I realize that Lucas is staring at me insistently, as if looking for answers. Then his gaze moves to Matt, who meets his eye, but doesn't seem inclined to indulge him. It seems the pissing contest is underway again. Those two are impossible! Could they *be* any more obstinate? I look away and turn my attention to Chloé, who gets off the bike and comes over to me.

"You okay, Charlotte? You seem… annoyed or something. Did you get up on the wrong side of the bed? Is there something I should know?"

"We'll talk about it later, Chloé. When we have some privacy."

"Sure thing, sweetie."

We decide to go and visit Terrence in the hospital before we start our day. Walking down the long, winding corridors, looking for room 294, my blood slowly turns to ice, as if my whole body remembers this suffocating, clinical smell. The blinking lights of the fire doors, the constant comings and goings of the staff, the sound of trolleys loaded with medical equipment. The atmosphere takes me back months. I can hardly breathe. I walk on robotically, following everyone, but I feel trapped in a state of lethargy. All I can hear is a dull hum. All other sounds seem muffled and distant.

"Charrrliiie!"

Before I can figure out who's talking to me, my head starts spinning, and I lean against the wall, stupefied, trying not to collapse in the middle of the corridor.

"Charlie, breathe! Breathe slowly. It'll pass. It's all over now! Breathe…"

Chloé is holding me up, with one arm under my armpit, trying to ease my panic. I hear fast footsteps coming towards us, and I feel Matt's warm hand on my face, but I can't move. My whole body is shaking. He hoists me up into his arms, and I hear Chloé ordering him to get me out of here. I let him carry me, nestled in his arms, powerless and relieved.

I feel instantly better once we're outside in the fresh air, and I gradually reconnect with my surroundings. Chloé is right next to me, her face solemn. Matt sits down on a bench and sits me on his knee, refusing to let me go.

"Dammit, Chloé, what's wrong with her?"

"She… She has an aversion to hospitals, but I didn't think it would have this bad of an effect on her, Matt," she explains hesitantly.

"Why didn't she say anything?"

Chloé plants herself in front of him haughtily, hands on hips, standing bolt upright.

"Undoubtedly because she had other things on her mind, Matt. I don't think she realized the effect coming here would have on her. Maybe you could tell me why she seemed so distracted earlier?"

I try to move. I'm still really dizzy, but I don't feel like listening to the two of them argue. Chloé, ever the quintessentially loyal friend, has skillfully directed Matt's attention away from the real reason for me almost fainting. "It's okay, I… I'm fine. I'm starting to feel better now. Stop squabbling!"

"Are you sure? Do you want to go home?"

"Of course I'm sure! We're not going to let a little dizzy spell spoil our day."

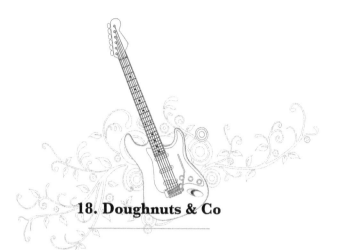

18. Doughnuts & Co

When the boys come out of the hospital, they are all worried about me. They tell me Terrence is doing well. He'll be going home this afternoon. Apparently, the accident wasn't too bad, and he escaped with just a few grazes on his head, nothing too serious. As we leave, Sam is as excited as a puppy at the prospect of the day ahead. He can be a real kid sometimes!

I can't help smiling as he tells us all which rides he's going to go on. An hour later, we arrive at the car park right next to the carnival. What a fantastic place! The second we are out of our cars, the smell of sugar and other fairground foods hits our nostrils and makes our mouths water. Chloé and I give each other a knowing look: given our respective sweet teeth, we know we'll be buying something from the first stand we see.

We go in and our senses are immediately assaulted by the pandemonium of rides, wild screams, and music: everything that makes this place such a hoot.

The first ride on our left is charmingly called "The Dominator." It spins its twelve riders 360 degrees, with impressive acceleration. Techno music throbs in the background, and judging by the faces of the people on board, it is hair-raising, to say the least… Not my idea of a party.

Sam drags Chris, Tommy, and Lucas onto the torture device. "Come on, get on! Don't be spoilsports!"

Matt answers him with a smile, "Go on, have fun! Just have it without me. And I don't think Charlie fancies being shaken all over the place after her dizzy spell. I'll stay with her."

He turns to Chloé and asks her if she wants to join the others.

"No, I think I'll start with something a little more mellow!"

"Chicken!" Sam hollers.

My friend's eyes instantly narrow to almost imperceptible slits. If there's one thing I know about my Chloé, it's that she's a real hothead. And it's not a good idea to bait her.

"Okay, I'm going! I bet you 'SAMinator' barfs when we get off!"

"Ha ha ha! You're on!" Matt exclaims.

We watch them disappear into the long line of people and take their seats. Matt is holding me in his arms, his hands clasped in front of my stomach. When the ride starts moving, its arms begin to swing, and each seat spins on its axis. It moves higher and higher, faster and faster, before stopping dead in the air and dropping towards the ground at breakneck speed. Just watching is enough to make my stomach twerk around inside me like Lady Luscious's butt.

Matt can't stop laughing: the guys' faces are so funny it hurts! They all look like they are about to die. Chloé, on the other hand, seems to be having the time of her life. When the ride finally slows to a stop, we move aside to let everyone off. Our gleeful gang emerges, all greener than a bunch of frogs, except for Chloé, who is bright eyed and bushy-tailed, a smile plastered across her face.

"OOOoooh maaaan!!! I'm... I'm gonna p... Blaargh..."

And with that, Saminator kindly shares the contents of his stomach with us in... 54 seconds. Record time! Yes, there's no denying it, Sam's a real champion.

Chloé doesn't deprive herself of the pleasure of teasing him, even while he is still doubled over, and the others join in enthusiastically.

"Right, what ride shall we go on next?" she asks him.

"Blaaaaargh..."

And he's off for round two. It'll be a while before he goes on another ride. We keep exploring, strolling around slowly, enjoying the ambiance. As we are passing a snack stand, our eyes are automatically drawn to the doughnuts.

"Fancy something sweet, kitten?" Matt murmurs in my ear, smiling.

Although I know his question leaves room for interpretation, I look at him and grin. "Yes, I fancy a nice, big…"

"Hell, just hearing you say that turns me on. Please tell me you didn't mean what you said earlier? About a week of abstinence and all that…"

I look him straight in the eye.

"A nice, big doughnut!" I say with confidence.

He bites his bottom lip and closes his eyes, trying to control himself in the face of my non-answer. We order our food and keep walking around, having a great time.

Chris and Tommy have found their fall guy for the rest of the day, and they don't give Sam a moment's peace.

Between two mouthfuls of doughnut, Matt kisses me, supposedly to get the sugar off my lips, but the kiss attacks continue, even a good ten minutes after I have finished eating.

Chloé and the boys decide to go on another ride, except for Sam that is, who just grumbles to himself. Matt suggests we check out the hall of mirrors: it's not scary and it's an attraction I've always loved. Sam gets over his sulkiness and comes with us.

We get our tickets and start exploring the labyrinth of windows and curved mirrors like crazy little kids. About five minutes in, I suddenly find myself separated from Matt. I work my way as strategically as possible around the meandering maze of optical illusions. When I get to the end of the corridor, I see Matt through a window. I watch him attentively, enjoying the fact that he hasn't seen me—this way I can take in every detail. Wow, this guy has got under my skin as easily as a scalpel. I stand there, glued to the spot, unable to take my eyes off him. Suddenly, he turns around, looks up, and our eyes meet. He walks forward, his steely gaze locked onto mine. Soon, he's standing right in front of me, but we are separated by a pane of glass. I can sense his frustration when he places his hand on the window, as if he's trying to touch me. I mirror him, my hand meeting his on the other side of the glass. We enjoy this private moment, just the two of us, looking at each other as though we were meeting for the first time. I press my forehead against the window, my eyes still deep in his. We stay like this for a moment, then he motions for me to walk along the wall so that we can reunite.

A few short minutes later, we meet up and find our way out. We have barely stepped through the door when he sweeps me up into his arms and takes me a few yards further away.

He takes a red thread out of his pocket, attaches one end to my little finger, and the other to his.

"There's no way I'm letting us get separated again, kitten."

My heart swells, and I smile, amused by this creative little gesture.

He squeezes me tightly and gives me a gentle kiss. Suddenly, Sam barges over. "Hey there, lovebirds! Shall we hit the road, or are you planning on making us a carnival baby?"

"God you're a drag once you've emptied your guts, Sam!" Matt retorts. "Alright already, we're coming!"

The rest of the group is a few yards away, in front of some sort of attraction. We go over to them and see that it is a kind of knock down game. The idea is that someone sits on a plank over a pool of water, while the others try to hit a lever with foam balls, to make them fall in.

The prizes are extravagant, and I fall in love with a giant pale pink rabbit.

"You want it, sweetheart?"

"It's gorgeous!"

"Sam, up for the challenge?"

Regaining his cocky demeanor, Sam swaggers off to sit on the plank. Matt untangles himself from me, arms himself with a few balls, throws and misses.

Chloé gives Sam a wicked grin. I'm sure those two have got some kind of score to settle. I just don't know what it is exactly.

She turns to me and in a sweet voice says, "You want the bunny rabbit?"

I nod. She knows I'm crazy about stuffed animals. I adore them. I'm such a kid!

"Okay, sweetie! Leave it to the expert."

Matt tries a second throw, but misses again. His failure earns him much mockery from Sam, who teases him for all he's worth.

"Hey, Matt, do you even have any eyes in those sockets, man?!"

That's when Chloé intervenes with a devious remark.

"Tell me, Sam, where were your eyes when Charlie was getting undressed the other morning?"

Sam's face crumples instantly, going from green, to red, to white. Matt's expression changes just as quickly, and his eyes narrow to imperceptible slits.

"You're a dead man, Sam!"

He throws his ball with the force of a cannon, and Sam drops straight into the water. Determined to throw a scare into Sam, Matt lunges at him. Sam desperately tries to explain himself. "No, dammit, I swear, I didn't see anything! Not a thing! Shit!"

I go over to my enraged lion and pull him to me, while Sam makes his soggy way out of the pool. Chris, Tommy and Lucas are in stitches, and Chloé does a little victory dance.

Still, I need to calm Simba down at some point. We collect my enormous stuffed animal, whom I dub Mister Water Rabbit, as a souvenir of our day. Matt, thrilled to be united again, crushes me against his chest.

It's almost 6 PM, and we decide to end the day with a visit to the haunted house. We all go into the Manor of Deadly Death, and as Matt passes Sam, he takes the opportunity to slap him on the back of the head.

But I've pretty much had enough of their bickering. "Hey! Give it a rest, okay! Matt, that's enough! Just calm down for crying out loud! You're not going to spend the rest of the day trying to pop him one!"

"I don't know, I quite like the sound of that!"

"No, seriously, you have to relax. He didn't see anything!"

"Hey, I know what would help me relax."

"Oh yeah, what's that? Beating the crap out of him?"

"No! Show me the stars…"

"What?"

"In your bedroom! Show me the stars. I want to sleep with you tonight. Under the stars! I promise I'll behave. I'll be as good as gold! Cross my heart…"

"This I've gotta see! Okay then. Alright. You can sleep at my place tonight."

He buries a kiss in my neck, savoring his victory, and we follow the others inside.

19. Home Sweet Home

It must be nearly seven when we leave the carnival, and we all decide to go get something to eat. Lucas finds himself sitting in the back of the SUV. He has kidnapped Mister Rabbit Water and is clamping him to his chest. Within a few minutes, he has fallen asleep, and the scene is well worth a selfie. Beneath his rebellious persona, Lucas is a really solid, loyal guy. Seeing him slumbering in the arms of a giant rabbit is too cute, I can't resist snapping a picture.

Matt gives me relaxed smile. Despite their sometimes stormy relationship, it's obvious that he has a lot of respect for Lucas. "How long have you two known each other?"

"I've known Lucas since we were kids, and I used to spend my holidays here. He's the closest thing I've got to a brother. Even though he can go from mildly annoying to completely unbearable in the blink of an eye, and even though he sometimes makes iffy decisions, I wouldn't change him for the world. And he really respects you, which is saying something: he's not the kind to make close friends, particularly with a girl. He's way too unsociable and fierce for that."

"Yeah, well, it doesn't always show, but it's clear you guys adore each other. I really like him. He always seems to know the right thing to say, and he gives great advice. What about the others? How did you meet them?"

"Well, Lucas and I used to go bowling whenever I was in France, and we met this bunch of lunatics at a tournament. We competed against them in the finals, and ended up really hitting it off. So we got into the habit of practicing with them every time I was in town. When I moved here, we became even closer. So there you have it, we're more than a team. Like I said, we're like family."

"And Sam?"

"Sam... Ha! That pain in the neck. That's another story! Where do I start? Well, Terrence is my uncle. I met Sam when I was having a meal with Terrence's parents. After dinner, we decided to go out for a drink with Terrence. Sam was cool, so we asked him to join us. That night, we ran into a group of jerks who were dead set on getting us wound up. Things got out of hand, and we ended up fighting. Sam threw himself into the fray and helped us without a second thought, and without him, we would have been goners, because they had us outnumbered. But he was like a ferocious, rabid dog! He's stuck with us ever since! Our very own Saminator!"

"Wow, quite the dream team!"

Once we found a parking spot, we all set off on foot as a group, looking for a nice restaurant. We choose a Breton *crêperie*, guided by our thirst for *chouchen:* a kind of mead made by fermenting honey in apple juice.

Sitting around the table, we admire the traditional decor: a gigantic *Gwenn ha Du*, the Breton flag, covers the back wall. The placemats are decorated with triskelion motifs, and the tankards on the shelves give the place a unique charm. The Celtic music by Adrian von Ziegler is like something straight out of the Middle Ages, softly filling the room to create a relaxing atmosphere.

"Ladies, fill up our glasses and let the feast begin!" Sam suddenly exclaims, caught up in the fun.

Chloé, being the ardent, independent woman she is, smacks him on the back of the head. "Man, if I cut it off and shove it down your throat, you won't be doing any feasting!"

Everyone guffaws and Sam gives Chloé a contrite smile. Those two are forever goading each other, but they seem to thrive on it!

We order our food, and it's a pleasant evening, with lots of revelry and laughter.

The meal finishes with a few glasses of *chouchen*. The

alcohol works its magic, and we leave in high spirits. Everyone says goodbye, and we are getting ready to head back to the apartment, when I see Sam and Chloé deep in conversation.

While we wait for my friend, Matt leans against a wall and pulls me to him, his arms instantly sending a shiver through my body.

"Are you cold?"

"No, I'm fine, just a little tipsy."

He gives me cheeky smile and tightens his grip.

When Chloé joins us, she is followed by Sam, who appears to be in seventh heaven. It seems there will be four of us sleeping at the apartment tonight... Matt gives me a knowing look, and entwines his fingers around mine as we meander down the sidewalk.

When we get home, we realize that it's already eleven. Time flies when you're having fun! It was such a great evening, and I didn't once look at my watch. At this rate, I'll be a sleep-deprived zombie by the end of the week!

We retire to our respective bedrooms, and I explain two or three elements of the fresco on the ceiling to Matt. "You'll understand what I was saying about the phosphorescent paint the other day when we turn off the light."

"Where did you get the idea?"

"I've spent a lot of time taking refuge in this room. I needed to create a space for myself where I would feel safe, but not trapped. During the day, I have a beautiful, sunny sky above me, and at night, I can look at the stars."

He gazes at me for a long instant, then turns his attention to the ceiling, examining every detail.

I can't help but smile at how enraptured he is by my painting. I head back to the kitchen to get a bottle of water.

Chloé is there, on the same mission, with her head in the fridge.

"I didn't realize it was so late. Tomorrow morning is going to be rough!" Chloé says.

"I need to go to the supermarket. The cupboards are starting to look as bare as the Sahara."

"What a crazy bunch, though! Didn't we have a great time today?"

"Amazing! And I love my rabbit! Thank you. But you went a bit far, poor Sam…"

"Don't feel sorry for him. He likes it. He encourages it, even! You must have lots of laughs at work, Charlie, but tell me something. Doesn't the boss mind his employees getting chummy with each other?"

"Well… I don't think he has a problem with it at all, given that the boss is getting chummy on my bed as we speak."

"Shit, are you kidding me? Matt? Wow! Seriously?"

I watch her as she chokes on her astonishment, and I nod.

"So that's what you were frowning about this morning? Was that it?"

"Yes. I'd just found out."

"And how did you react?"

"Badly. I'll explain later, though. Do you mind? I'm exhausted."

"No worries! I'm worn out too. Sleep well. Well, try to, anyway!" she snickers.

When I get back into my bedroom, Matt is lying on the bed, wearing only black boxers, with his arms behind his head. He's still looking at my painting, seemingly lost in contemplation.

He's to die for! He gives me a naughty look. Caught in the act of ogling! He knows the effect he has on me, and he loves to exploit it, recklessly and mercilessly. I stride over to my closet and take out a massive T-shirt, which I put on where he can't see me, hidden behind the door. Once I have changed, I turn off the light and join him to watch the star-spangled sky emerge.

He gasps, pulling me to him in a possessive gesture.

"Wow! It's as beautiful as the fireflies dancing over the lake! You're so amazing. So talented! It's like sleeping in a wonderland. You really should think about exhibiting your art."

As he enthuses about my work, his hands stroke my lower back with consummate kindness, sweeping away my earlier resolve. A deliciously warm sensation builds in my lower abdomen as he caresses me, and when his fingers skim the lace of my panties, it's clear from my breathing that he's hit his mark.

"Matt…"

"Mmmm?"

"What do you think you're doing?"

"Caressing you…"

"I think we had an agreement, didn't we?"

"No! I don't think that was part of the deal. How could it be? I said I'd be as good as gold, and I'm the one being punished, not you… so technically, there's no reason for me not to give you pleasure…"

"Matt, seriously, you're impossi— Oooh…"

His fingers are teasing my inner thighs, venturing under the elastic of my panties to seek out my sensitive flesh. His mouth on my neck strengthens the surge of immodest pleasure.

"No, don't… Oooooh, fuck, Matt!"

"Is there a problem?"

When his finger delicately blushes my clitoris, my breath catches in my throat, and I'm overcome by the most marvelous sensation. He teases it, torments it, gratifying it just enough with his languorous rhythm. I feel myself slipping into a world where my senses have only one master: Matt.

He sits up so that he is towering over me, and positions himself between my thighs so he can slide down my lacy defenses. His hands part my knees.

He keeps the pace slow, lingering patiently, savoring every part of my throbbing intimacy, reining in his own desire to satisfy mine. My heart beats wildly in my chest, abandoning its rhythm to chaos, and I struggle to silence my moans.

His eyes are gleaming with satisfaction as he moves around behind me, carefully placing a hand over my mouth while he penetrates me with two fingers, his thumb rubbing my clitoris dangerously. As my body begins to writhe, he responds by moving his fingers faster, accompanying my unbridled pleasure with his hand, so that my orgasm explodes through me, so strong it seems to radiate beyond my body.

My cries are lost in the palm of his hand, which he keeps tightly over my mouth, a victorious smile curling the corners of his lips. My body trembles with the aftershock of this earthquake. He holds me against him, buries his face in my neck, and sprinkles little kisses along my ear, waiting for my breathing to return to normal.

Quick check-up:
Resolve: weak!
Brain: lost
State: XXXXXX
Heart: fully trained and tamed
Matt: top marks

"You okay?"

"Please tell me that's a rhetorical question!"

He laughs and rolls on top of me, propping himself up on his elbows, his face just inches from mine. He brushes my lips with his, gently nibbles them, then kisses them lightly. I clamp my hands behind his neck and pull him to me for a deeper, slower kiss, tangling my fingers in his hair, tasting those mind-blowing lips. After this mind-blowing kiss, he lies down beside me, I curl up in his arms, and we set our sights on dreamland. Just before I drop off, I hear him whispering a few words that make my heart leap. "I love loving you under the stars..."

Drunk on each other, we finally let sleep consume us.

20. Tickled

Our early morning peace is disturbed by the sound of groaning and grunting. What? We don't have any animals... The noises get louder and louder, and there's no doubt where they're coming from. What the hell is she doing to him to make him howl like that? I am just wondering whether or not she is biting his balls and viciously scratching him when Matt rolls onto his side and curls his body around mine.

"Right, I'm gonna make him pay for this!"

Matt's sleepy grumbling sends me into fits of giggles, and I know that the real reason for his bad mood is the punishment he suffered last night. Hearing Sam's throaty cries is only rubbing it in. I chuckle and rub his head. "Is there a problem, Matt?"

"Yes, a big one. Or rather a huge one, a gigantic problem..."

He grabs my hand and guides it to his rock-hard erection. Yes, his gigantic problem is there for me to feel in all its glory.

"I'm going to explode if he doesn't stop all that moaning!"

He buries his head in the pillow and growls with frustration.

I can't help but laugh at his obvious despair. Suddenly, Matt flips over, and before I can react he is straddling me, immobilizing my hips with his thighs.

"You think this is funny? Seriously? You think it's funny? How about this? Is this funny?"

He starts tickling me, his lips curling into a wicked smile. Hysterical, I writhe and wriggle and squirm, trying to escape his grasp, squealing with laughter as I battle for freedom. I manage to fight my way free, and I leap out of the bed. "No, no, stop, I can't take any more, I—"

"I can't take any more either, come here!"

He starts chasing me around the bedroom. I jump over the bed, grab a cushion, and throw it at him. Even when he is laughing so hard he can hardly breathe, his predator's instinct is perfectly honed, and he continues to give chase. Soon, the pillow fight is in full swing. We have turned into two hysterical kids! The feather war has been declared, and every cushion in reach becomes a projectile. Matt pounces and manages to pin me against the wall, knocking the table lamp over along the way. With one hand under each buttock, he lifts me up and pushes my back against the wall. I wrap my legs around his hips as he kisses me furiously.

"Bad kitty!"

I smile, trapping his lip between my teeth and giving it a gentle bite before running the tip of my tongue along it.

"Dammit, that's not fair! You…"

"I…?"

"A week? That's inhumane! Can't we negotiate? Let's say… Wednesday?"

I pout, taking great pains to really make him suffer. He tries sliding his mouth down my neck, trailing his tongue over my skin, kneading one of my breasts and titillating the nipple, pinching it, stroking it, sending electric shocks through my entire body. "No, Matt, you're cheating. You… Ooooh… I said…"

"Say yes! Wednesday! Say yes!"

Between the caresses and the powerful erection rammed between my legs, I can't take it any longer. "Yes, yes, Wednesday! Okay!" I gasp.

He lets me go and carefully lowers me to the floor, his chest puffed out victoriously.

"Hungry?"

◎ ◎ ◎

We walk out of the bedroom and into the kitchen, where Chloé and Sam are already making breakfast. If you ignore the fact that Sam is only wearing boxers and Matt is shooting daggers at him, everything is great!

"The next time I hear you braying at dawn, I'll tear your testicles off, got that?"

Sam flinches defensively and miserably tries to defend himself. "It's not my fault! For your information, sleeping with Cruella isn't exactly restful, especially when she wakes up with twisted urges! I kid you not, man, you have no idea what I've been through!"

Chloé whacks him on the back of the head and gives him a look that could kill.

"That's from Cruella, dickhead!"

Matt and I look at each other in astonishment, struggling to understand the bizarre dynamics of their relationship. Knowing Chloé, I get the impression she isn't entirely innocent. "Fess up, Chloé, what did you do to poor Sam?"

"Nothing! I looked after him, that's all. Nothing to make a fuss about!"

"Nothing to make a fuss about?" Sam screeches, "Are you kidding? Wampa here thought waxing my chest would be a good way to draw me from my slumber! I woke up with sticky strips all over it!"

"Oh, get over yourself, Sam, that happens to us all the time, in much more sensitive places! Actually, come to think of it…"

"Never in a million years! Is your friend out of her mind? She really has a screw loose! If you come anywhere near my crown jewels with your damned wax strips, I swear, you'll regret it!"

What is happening? We seem to be drifting in a fourth dimension, but the laughter that overcomes us is as intense as it is uncontrollable.

We are literally crying with laughter, doubled over at the sight of Sam completely terrorized by Chloé, who gives me an evil wink. The woman is hilarious! I love her!

"What? Charlie, admit it, they're nicer without hair!" she says, convincingly.

Matt gets up, wraps his arms around Chloé and squeezes her tight. "Free drinks at the pub for you... for life!!!"

"Umm, yes, on that subject, Mister Boom Boom, I hear you're the big boss?"

"Hmm, yes, true…"

"You could have told her before!"

"Okay, Chloé, I'm already being punished for that! Sam isn't the only one being made to suffer, you know."

"Ha, I don't believe that, after the earthquake you regaled us with this morning! Tell us, what was going on in your bedroom? World War III?"

"Not far off, Chloé, not far off…"

Matt turns to me and gives me a complicit smile.

"Mister Boom Boom? Interesting!" Sam says sadly. "But it doesn't change the fact that my chest been waxed bare…"

◎ ◎ ◎

A few days later, I start work on Mission Halloween. I'm really excited about planning the decorations, my costume, and goodies for the party!

I have just under twenty days to get everything organized, and I already have a very clear idea of what I want to suggest to Terrence.

I start making a list of the supplies I'll need, and sketch the mural that I want to paint across several wooden boards. It will be a panoramic cemetery scene with coffins opening and bare trees under a disturbing moon: a really creepy landscape. I think it could really transform the pub for the event. I plan to use shades of gray and earthy colors to accentuate the dingy atmosphere of the graveyard.

I think I can find everything I need in a store in town, which has lots of hangings, candles, masks and more.

My vivid imagination allows me to see precisely where I'm going with this. When the front door slams, I see Chloé charging into the apartment like a furious fireball. I put down my felt-tip pen and stare at her in surprise. "Is something wrong, hon?"

She sits on the bed, then flops down onto the mattress and stretches out, her eyes glued to the ceiling.

"Yes, Sam!"

"Oh, are you two battling over body hair again?"

She laughs. "No, but he's driving me mad," she says in a pensive voice. "Last time I saw him, he told me he was too busy to meet me this week, and just now, as I was leaving work, I ran into him with another woman."

"Oh shit, but... Were they close?"

"I... I don't know, I saw red and left before he noticed me."

"Maybe she's just a friend!"

"So why not just tell me, instead of leaving me in the dark?"

"I don't know, but you should talk to him about it."

She gets off the bed and leans over my shoulder, examining my sketch.

"Let's see... Oh! That's so cool! What is it?"

"The scenery for the Halloween party."

I start telling her about my ideas and the atmosphere I'm looking to create, which leads to a long discussion on the subject. She gives me a few ideas, but we are pretty much on the same wavelength, and we work together to plan it all out.

"Now for the costumes!" she adds, brimming with excitement. "What have you chosen?"

"I'm not sure yet, but—"

"Ooh! I know! Let's go look for costumes together. Come on, Charlie! It'll be great fun. And it will help me come up with an action plan for this situation with Sam."

I smile to myself at the thought of her action plan. If I had one piece of advice to give Sam, it would be: "Good luck! Run fast! Run far!"

"That's a brilliant idea!"

"Let's go!"

21. A Maiden and a Black Cat

When we get to the costume superstore, we scour the long shelves displaying all kinds of items.

This should keep us busy for the rest of the afternoon!

We take our time, trying on vampire false teeth, witch's hats, capes, and other accessories. When we get to the costumes, there is an embarrassment of riches! Outfit after outfit, each more fabulous than last. I didn't think we would find so many great costumes. I can't believe it! This is not going to be an easy decision. "Chloé, what kind of thing were you thinking of?"

"No idea, but I'm sure we'll find just the thing here!"

We keep looking. We are giggling and chatting when Chloé's attention is suddenly drawn to a latex Catwoman suit.

"Check this out. I'm sure it would look great on you!"

"You can forget about that right now. There's no way I'm wearing that thing!"

"Oh, go on! It's sooo cool!"

"No, not on your life! Why don't *you* wear it if you like it so much?"

"Okay. Sold. I'll be Catwoman! I want a whip!"

I suddenly feel very sorry for Sam. I'm half-worried, half-amused. "Oh God! Poor Sam!"

"Right, now let's find you a killer costume, Charlie!"

My phone rings, interrupting our madness. "Hello, Matt?"

"Where are you? I went to your place, but there's nobody home!"

"I'm out shopping with Chloé. We're on a hunt for our Halloween costumes!"

"Oh damn, I need to find one too! What are you wearing?"

"Not sure yet, but Chloé has chosen her costume, and I'd advise Sam to be on his best behavior."

"Go on, spill the beans!"

"No, it's a surprise!"

"I guess I'll just have to be patient, then. Listen, I have to go away. They just told me. I should be back by the end of the week."

"Um, where are you going?"

"It's for work, there are things I need to do. I'll call you as soon as I get back, okay?"

"Okay!"

I hang up, and my face falls. Chloé instantly knows that Matt has to go away again, and she slings an arm around my shoulders.

"Don't worry, Charlie. He's crazy about you! Come on, we've still got some shopping to do."

She takes me down the next aisle, and suddenly stops in front of a costume. "Oh! Charlie, I've found it!"

She pulls it off the rack and grabs my hand, dragging me towards the fitting rooms. "Put this on, immediately."

She stuffs the costume into my hands, and pushes me into the dressing room, picking up a stunning pair of boots to go with her own outfit.

As soon as I come out of the stall, Chloé shrieks with delight and does a ridiculous celebratory dance.

"Matt is going to burst out of his pants, honey!"

I walk over to the mirror, and freeze when I see my reflection.

The outfit is sumptuous and decadent. A steampunk version of Little Red Riding Hood. Wow! In an outfit like this, the Big Bad Wolf would have eaten her up in an entirely different way!

It's a very short white cotton dress, the skirt of which boasts three frilly layers. The first layer is covered with blood red velvet, and the other two are immaculately white, falling well above the knee and showing off a good portion of my thighs.

Over the top, I am wearing a brown corset with three straps running sideways across it, showing off the low-cut neckline of the dress. It laces up to cinch in my waist, giving the outfit a hint of rock 'n' roll. Two more straps hanging down from the waist like suspenders hold up the frills, giving a wave effect at the front and dropping to the knees at the back. The brown, high-heeled boots are made to look like leather lace, and they hug my shapely legs perfectly.

And the finishing touch: a red velvet cape. "Whoa, Chloé, it's way too short!"

"You'll have him drooling!"

"May I remind you I'm working that evening?"

"Then they'll all be drooling! It's perfect!"

In the end, I have to admit this costume really is fantastic, and I give in.

We continue our shopping, and Chloé adds a black velvet choker to my outfit, with little chains hanging from it in arcs. It is delicately embellished with an iridescent white stone mounted in the center.

Once we have everything we need, we take advantage of our girly time to visit a lingerie store that has opened next door. And the spending continues, neither of us able to resist the gorgeous lingerie sets.

◎ ◎ ◎

When we get back to the apartment at around seven, we have a quick bite to eat before I go to work. I take the first chance I get to tell Terrence about my ideas and show him my sketch. He's immediately on board, and gives me a generous budget for everything. I will probably go and buy the last few decorations tomorrow. I saw some things I wanted in the store, and I need to get the planks for my mural.

Lucas offers to come with me, to help me carry everything, and we agree to meet the next morning at ten. It's a pretty quiet evening, and we finish up early. I am back at the apartment by 11:30 PM. I get a text from Matt shortly thereafter, telling me that he's going to bed and he's thinking of me. I tell him about my plans with Lucas for the next day, and we send each other kisses good night.

◎ ◎ ◎

Lucas comes over the next morning at ten on the dot, and we have a quick cup of coffee before we head out. He's in a good mood, but I can't stop looking at the bruise on his face.

"What's that?" I can't help asking, narrowing my eyes. "Trying out some new makeup?"

"Don't worry, it's no big deal, Charlie."

"Hey, don't try that with me, Lucas!"

I reach out and brush my fingertips over his black eye, but he flinches and makes a face—not a good sign. "Right, you're not getting out of this. Show me!"

"Charlie, it's nothing. It's…"

I step towards him and slowly lift up his sweater. My jaw drops: his torso is badly scraped from his groin to his pecs. And the injuries look recent. His skin is burned in places, as if he's been dragged across the tarmac. Shit! "LUCAS! What happened?!"

"I told you, Charlie, it's nothing. I just skidded on my motorbike…"

"Skidded? Do you think I'm stupid? From the looks of you, your run-in with the road was pretty violent!"

"Listen, I'm used to it. It's… Dammit, you don't give up, do you? Okay, I was going a bit fast… But that's my problem."

"What *is* your problem, exactly?"

"I have no limits! That's just how I am. End of story!"

"If you say so, but you're not leaving before I've cleaned this mess up!"

"Okay, take advantage of my body if that's what you want!"

"You jerk!"

He smiles proudly, and pulls off his sweater.

Lucas! Man, he is a real cheeky little devil! I shoot him a furious look and go about repairing the damage.

After that, we go shopping, and I am really glad that Lucas is there with me to help. It's a laugh a minute, and in the end, we manage to get everything on my list in under three hours. I ask him if he feels like eating at my place and watching the *Star Wars* saga, like we promised we would.

Stretched out on the sofa, we revel in our choice like two kids, armed with a big bowl of popcorn. When Chloé comes home, she has Sam with her, and at the sight of Lucas spread out on my sofa, his eyes grow wide with surprise.

"Fuck man! You've got balls of steel! If Matt finds you here…"

I intervene before he goes any further down the rabbit hole, "Sam, chill out, Matt knows very well I was with Lucas today. We went shopping for Halloween decorations!"

Sam spins around to face Chloé. "Ah yes, Halloween, what are you going as, Chloé?"

"Your worst nightmare!"

"As long as you don't bring your wax strips, I'm fine with it!"

Lucas gapes at us in confusion, totally lost. "Anyone care to enlighten me?" he asks, intrigued. "What's all this about wax strips?"

Sam is quick as lightning with his answer, "Ask this madwoman," he says, nodding towards Chloé, who in response to his verbal attack, throws the contents of her glass in his face.

"Whaaaaa? What the…? What did I say?"

I watch Sam dripping on the floor, and hand him a towel, then catch the giggles from Lucas, who is in fits of laughter on the sofa. "If you ask me, Sam, you should be careful with what you say. If you keep talking like that, you'll end up with balls like Kojak's head! So if you value your body hair and your life, I'd stop calling Chloé a madwoman, Cruella, and all the other lovely nicknames you've come up with for her."

Lucas, still doubled up with laughter, raises an eyebrow and says, "Is it always this much fun at your place? Because if it is, I'd love to come over more often!"

The four of us finally end up eating together, then the boys go off to work, and I make the most of my evening off. I grill Chloé for details about her and Sam, "So, did you talk to him? Is it all worked out?"

"No, he doesn't even know I saw him with that girl."

"What? But I thought you were going to ask him about it."

"I will… later. Right now, I'm preparing my revenge."

"Chloé, what are you plotting?"

She smiles, and I could swear I see little red horns growing out of her head.

"He's going to learn how to behave himself, I'll tell you that!"

Poor Sam, his suffering is far from over.

Matt calls me later that evening, but we don't talk for long. We are interrupted when a man comes looking for him. "We need you. We're waiting for you!" I hear the man say.

He apologizes, and I let him get back to his duties, annoyed that he is being stolen away from me again.

After hanging up, I sit there, puzzled. I'm not the clingy type, but with Matt, I realize I am ticking all the boxes of the pathetic, love-sick girl.

22. Co-conspirators and Confidants

The next day, I get up early, determined to get started on my Halloween panorama. I get all my things out, inhale my coffee, then get down to work.

I let my paintbrushes run free, soaking up the distinctive smell of solvent, transferring every detail of my sketch. I am totally absorbed in my work: this always happens when I paint. I become one with my art, and being in this bubble helps me forget my worries. Every detail, every shadow needs my full attention. I devote myself to tracing the contour of the moon, making it glow with hints of blue. Inside it, you can see a haunting face, veiled in mist.

The further I get with my painting, the happier I am with the emerging result. My phone rings at one point and I answer robotically.

It's Lucas. His voice rips me from my reverie. "Hey, Charlie!"

"Hey, Lucas, everything, okay?"

"Umm, I was wondering if you'd be willing to play nurse for me again?"

"Don't tell me you've gone flying off your bike again?"

"Nope, no more accidents, but you really helped yesterday, and it's hurting a bit today. So… Well, I don't want to impose."

"You're not bothering me, Lucas. I'm happy to help. Come on over. How far away are you?"

The knock on the front door answers my question. I'm starting to think men have some sort of obsession with phoning from the doorstep.

I go to open it, and find Lucas with a bag of croissants, running a nervous hand through his hair. "Come in, you big doofus!"

He steps in, looking slightly ill at ease, and puts the bag down on the kitchen table.

"Is that your Halloween costume?"

I give him a puzzled look, then glance down and realize what I am wearing. In shorts and a tank top, with my hair held up by small, thin paintbrushes, I look like I've escaped from an insane asylum. I laugh loudly. "No, I'm painting the planks for the landscape."

"You've got paint on your nose!"

"Oh! Shit..."

I give my nose a good rub. "I wasn't expecting visitors," I say, smiling.

"Yeah... Sorry, Charlie."

"No worries. It's fine! I'll go get the antiseptic."

His wounds are looking better than yesterday. When I'm done cleaning them, I offer him some coffee and pour some for myself as well.

"Show me, Charlie!"

"What?"

"The planks..."

"Oh yeah! Sorry, my mind was elsewhere..."

He narrows his eyes and gives me a long, hard look, then surprises me with a question. "Do you miss him?"

I blush and look down. "Yes..."

"Don't worry, Charlie. He misses you too!"

"How can you be sure, Lucas?"

"I know him, and Matt, well... I've never seen him behave like this over a girl."

"But I have no idea what he's doing when he vanishes like this."

"He has commitments to honor, Charlie! You've just got to trust him!"

"I know, but it's... it's hard."

He nods. "So, what about these planks?"

"They're in the bedroom. Come on."

When Lucas sees the fresco, his jaw drops.

"They are not finished yet. I still need to do the trees and the coffins in the foreground, but you get the idea."

"It's... wow! Matt wasn't exaggerating about your talents, Charlie! This is amazing."

I explain in detail what else I'm going to paint, and express my doubts about the shape of the tree. "I can't decide whether to make the branches trail or fade out... I'm not sure which would look best."

He picks up the sketch, looks at it carefully, then asks me for a pencil. I hand him one. He turns to a blank page in my sketchbook and starts scribbling, glancing back and forth between the paper and my painting.

When he hands me his work, I can't hide my astonishment. That's no doodle! That's the work of an expert hand! I stare at him, stupefied, and then whistle in admiration. "Lucas! That's fantastic! Why didn't you tell me you could draw?"

"Because not many people know, that's all! I'm a very private person, as you well know by now."

"Good grief, you're stubborn! How about helping me finish this landscape?"

He looks at me with gleaming eyes, and then gives me a grin wide enough to split his face in half. "Yeah! I'd love to! Hey, Charlie..."

"Yes?"

"Matt's lucky. He's a real lucky bastard to have you!"

I blush, his compliment leaving me a little flustered. Lucas is a loner, a mad dog who takes foolish risks, but he's also a talented artist. I'm touched that he has opened up to me. It speaks to trust. In the space of a few weeks, we have gone from colleagues to co-conspirators and confidants. Seeing him show his true self today moves me to the brink of tears. He admitted that he is forever pushing the boundaries, and I guess that he takes these risks to fill the emptiness inside. He has an enormous heart, and I'm proud to be his friend.

When we finish the painting, it's after six.

We've spent the whole day on it, but the results are unbelievable. We have brought a dark, sinister atmosphere to life, somehow filling it with deep poetry. Tim Burton would be proud of us. Lucas has even added a skeleton wearing a top hat, which brings to mind the Mad Hatter in *Alice in Wonderland*.

"We did it, Charlie!"

"Yeah, nice work! I think it's going to look incredible once it's in place. You've got serious skills, Lucas."

"Well, it's like Théophile Gautier said: 'We paint with our hearts and minds more than with our hands…'"

I can't help but admire him. It must be hard work hiding who he really is. But one thing is certain: the girl who wins his heart will need infinite reserves of patience and a treasure trove of affection to tame this fiery, intrepid romantic.

"Right, I'd better go. See you later at the pub!"

"Okay, Lucas, and thanks."

"No, thank you, Charlie, for today. It's done me good."

After he leaves, I put everything away and get ready for the evening.

When I get to work, Chris and Tommy come over and hug me. I ask them if Terrence is around yet, but he's not. Damn… I wanted to talk to him about the pumpkins I wanted to carve: my kitchen is too small, so I was hoping to do it here. Oh well, I'll sort that out later. Matt calls me before I start my shift.

"I miss you! Did you have a good day?"

"I miss you too, Matt. When will you be back?"

"The day after tomorrow. I have to see a supplier, and then I'm coming home. What did you do today?"

"I painted with Lucas."

"Put him on!"

"But—"

"I said let me talk to him!"

I scan the room for Lucas, and when I spot him, I beckon him over. I hope I haven't got him into trouble. I hand him the phone, telling him Matt wants to talk.

"Hi, Matt! Yes… Yeah… Uh-huh… She misses you, you jerk! Well, fuck you… Yes… Yes… I know she's wonderful… Okay, I'll put her back on."

He hands the phone back to me. I take it, still trying to get my head around this bizarre exchange and figure out what his victorious expression is all about. "Hello?"

"Wow, way to go! That guy hasn't picked up a paintbrush in years! You're a real little miracle worker... My miracle worker!"

Relieved by his words, I release all the air I was holding in my lungs. I can't keep up with those two! We chat for a while longer, then I hang up and go back to work.

Later on, Terrence arrives and I seize the opportunity to explain my pumpkin idea. He's fine with it, and fine with me using the kitchen. He even says I can get the guys to help. An afternoon in the kitchen with that lot could be interesting to say the least, and I smile at the thought.

"So that's it, then, we're on pumpkin duty?" Chris calls out as I'm clearing a table.

"Oh, you don't have to come, Chris. That was Terrence's idea. I can manage perfectly well on my own."

"Hey, Charlie, we're a team. Anyway, it'll be fun. I'm not complaining, I can't wait! It will be my first pumpkin party."

"Really? You've never carved pumpkins for Halloween?"

"Umm, no. First time. I'll be losing my pumpkin virginity. Uh, that's a weird thing to say, right?"

"Right!"

As we valiantly try to keep straight faces, Sam, Lucas, and Tommy eye us suspiciously. "As it's your first time, I'll make you some Halloween treats to celebrate!"

"Oh God, yes! Hey, guys, just so you know, on pumpkin day, Charlie's cakes are for me, so hands off!!!"

"Is everything always a competition with you guys?"

"Always! It's how we are. We're all as stubborn as a bunch of bulls, as I'm sure you've noticed. But I'm the worst. Maybe my roots have got something to do with it..."

"Which are?"

"Hispanic. Andalusia. The Province of Malaga to be more precise."

"So that's where that little accent comes from!"

"Cute, isn't it? You love it, go on, admit it!"

"You're all the same! So damned sure of yourselves! Sure, it has its charm, Casanova!"

"Oh no, not Casanova, he was Italian. Are you trying to insult me? Call me Don Juan!"

"Don Juan? Hmm, let's see. How are your ankles? Not too swollen?"

"Not my ankles, no, but something else sure is…"

My mouth falls open in surprise as I register his lewd little remark, and I whack him with a dish towel, which only makes him laugh harder. "You dirty, perverted little scumbag!"

One is as shameless as the next. They're beyond help!

But I love it! They feel free to be themselves around me. They treat me like a friend, and they don't care that I'm a girl. They've completely accepted me into their madcap gang.

And that kind of real friendship knows no bounds.

23. Cookies and a Treat

Two days later, I am sitting at my kitchen table with a cup of coffee, flicking through books in search of baking ideas. I have my entire library of cookbooks piled up in front of me, and I work my way tirelessly through the pages, carefully itemizing each recipe. I would love to make several kinds of treats. I bookmark a handful of recipes, including miniature orange-cinnamon-cookie *tiramisù,* chocolate spider muffins, gingerbread skeletons, and lemon meringue pies with the meringue piped in the shape of ghosts. Filled with enthusiasm, I decide to make the gingerbread cookies now, because they will stay fresh.

I lay out all the ingredients needed for the recipe and follow the steps. I put my cookies in the oven, and when I get them out, I am delighted with the result. The shape is perfect. I just need to pipe the skeletons on top with white icing.

Just as I am getting ready to decorate my cookies, three little knocks at the door pull me away from my work. I quickly wipe my hands on my apron and go to see who's there.

It's Matt, holding Mister Rabbit Water in his arms! I fling my arms around his neck, delighted to see him. The last few days have felt endless!

"Hey, kitten, happy to see me?"

"Too happy!"

"You can never be too happy. God, I missed you! Why is your hair… white? And what's that smell? It's making my mouth water!"

"Oh, it must be flour in my hair. I've been baking for

Halloween. And Chris told me he'd never carved a pumpkin so we're going to celebrate his initiation, my way!"

"You're unbelievable! Can I have a taste?"

We walk into the kitchen, or rather Matt walks; I'm pretty much dangling from his neck, but he doesn't seem to mind. He leans towards the tray and goes to take a cookie, but I slap his hand away. "No, wait, they're not finished! You can try one when they're done. I promise. But just one, greedy guts!"

He pretends to sulk, and then sits me on the edge of the sink, lifting me up by my butt. He kisses my neck greedily and moans with pleasure.

"Let me taste you, then…"

"Right here?"

"Here, there, everywhere!"

"You're crazy!"

"Hmm… about you!"

"I've got a deal for you: help me finish and then we can do whatever you like."

The glint in his eye says he's not thinking Scrabble, a walk in the park or anything along those lines. No, I know that glint: it promises something much more exciting, and seeing this flame inside him sends frissons right through me. I'm pretty sure that even my panties are trembling!

Suddenly, he's raring to go. He grabs a spatula and a piping bag, and wields them in front of me impatiently.

"Come on, hurry up and get to work!"

We mess around like two silly kids for almost an hour, teasing each other: him innocently pinching my butt, me throwing flour at him. It's so good to see him again. When we finish piping the last skeletons, they look fantastic!

"They're absolutely perfect! We, however, are a total mess!"

Caked in flour and chocolate, we look positively frightful.

"You know what that means? I'm going to have to soap you up! Go on, get in the shower!"

He grabs me by the waist and pushes me towards the bathroom, which is less spacious than his, but still big enough for the two of us. We undress each other and step into the shower. It takes him less than ten seconds to pin me against the wall, at the mercy of his hungry mouth. His tongue plunges in to meet mine, rolling around in slow, carnal movements, possessive and voracious. My lust for him is out of control, and my hands work their way down to his vigorous cock, standing proud and hard against my thigh. He growls with pleasure when my fingers close around it, sliding back and forth in long, slow movements. My initiative takes him by surprise and his eyes widen, then his lips curl into a small smile. I can feel him trembling between my fingers as his hands knead my buttocks passionately. Feeling adventurous, I look him right in the eye and begin to kneel down in front of his hard erection, then I gently take it in my mouth.

"Fuck! Oh, shit…!"

I taste him, fanning the flames of his desire. I can feel him throbbing on my tongue as it caresses the soft skin of his cock, tasting it, teasing it, then taking it into my mouth completely. With his hands braced against the wall, he moans loudly, trying not to lose control. I move back and forth rhythmically, and his whole body seems to be fighting to contain his rising orgasm.

"I… Oh God, I don't think I can wait…"

"Mmmm, you don't have to…"

Putting an end to his agony, I quicken my pace until he spurts inside my mouth, releasing his explosive ecstasy into me.

I stand up and kiss him softly, linking my arms around his neck as he wraps his around my body and pulls me close. "I'm happy to see you…"

"So am I! You've done me in!"

"Great. One all. Right down the middle! Last time, I had all the fun!"

We silently lather each other down, liberally stroking and fondling each other. Then, I slip on a robe and Matt wraps a towel around his waist. We step out of the bathroom and come face to face with Sam and Chloé, who are on their way in the door.

"Well, well, don't let us disturb you! I guess you couldn't bear to be apart for ten minutes, so you just had to take a shower together?" Sam teases.

"Shut it, Sam, we're looking after the planet. SAV-ING E-NER-GY… Well, sort of!" Matt retorts.

○ ○ ○

Pumpkin carving day finally comes around, and we meet at the pub at 2 PM. I arrive with trays full of goodies, which I put down on the bar. Tommy immediately comes over to help, and Lucas goes to get the pumpkins out of the car. They all seem anxious to start carving, and their enthusiasm warms my heart.

Matt couldn't come. Another emergency to add to his long list of absences. Still, I don't pry. I want to trust him, and I tell myself that he'll tell me more when he's ready.

When I show them my baked goods, they all devour the contents of the trays with their eyes. It seems my decorating prowess is duly noted! They taste each of my creations, then taste them again, in ecstasy over the flavors.

Only Tommy has just one of each. "Not into sweets, Tommy?" I ask him, surprised.

"Yes, but I need to be careful."

"Careful? What do you mean? Don't tell me you're watching your weight?"

"Well, actually, yes. I have to, for the championships…"

"What championships?"

"Our Tommy is an accomplished athlete, Charlie!" Chris explains. "He's preparing for the boxing championships. You wouldn't believe how good he is!"

"Oh! Tommy! I had no idea! Congratulations!"

"I have to watch what I eat if I want to stay in the same weight class for my fights."

"Now I get it! Okay, guys, shall we get started?"

The next few hours go by in a haze of hilarity. In short, Sam is about as good with a pumpkin as an oyster with a rake, Lucas creates a masterpiece in the style of Tim Burton but which looks more like a zombie than a Jack-O'-Lantern, Tommy really makes an effort and tries to take it seriously, but fails, and Chris is like a kid in a sandbox!

There's a merry mess in the kitchen, with a totally slapstick vibe: there is pumpkin everywhere, but we're making progress… well, we're trying to.

With all our joking and clowning around, we don't finish our army of pumpkins until around six. Hard work, but well done!

Obviously, the boys have eaten everything I made, apart

from a few things I carefully put aside for Matt and Terrence. And it's lucky I did, or they wouldn't have gotten anything at all!

I tell the boys not to skimp on the elbow grease while I'm busy tidying up. "Come on, guys, this place looks like a pigsty! Move, move, move! Sam, can you put all this stuff away, bring me the utensils from behind the counter, and put the rest in my car?"

"No problem! And uh, Charlie..."

He comes over to me, shuffling from foot to foot. "What, do you need to use the little boys' room?"

"No, I need to talk to you!"

"Go on, Sam, I'm all ears!"

"Umm, well, I... I'd like to invite Chloé out to eat somewhere, but I can't figure out how to get through to her. She keeps giving me the cold shoulder. I get the feeling she's mad at me, but I don't know why."

"Have you tried talking to her and asking why she's angry?"

"Well, no..."

"Maybe you could try to be a little more... sensitive?"

Lucas bursts out laughing. "Not a chance!" he says gleefully. "Sam's about as sensitive as a bull in a china shop! Give it up, man. You don't stand a chance!"

"Dammit!"

Chloé obviously hasn't talked to him. And I must say, it doesn't bode well. She must be plotting her revenge. Suddenly, my heart goes out to poor Sam: it looks like Chloé is going to make him pay dearly.

24. Psyche and Cupid

That evening, I join Matt at his place. It's nice being with him again. Huddled together on the sofa, with a glass of wine in our hands, we talk about the guys, then about Sam and Chloé. I share my concerns about Chloé, and he laughs out loud, explaining that she is just what Sam needs. A hard-headed chick who knows how to handle him.

"So, tell me, what are you wearing for Halloween?"

"Oh, I should never have let Chloé talk me into buying that outfit. The more I think about it, the more I regret it."

"Why, don't you like it?"

"Oh, I love it, but you know, Chloé is more of an… extrovert than I am. And she's just a bit more… liberated."

"Are you trying to tell me it's sexy?"

I roll my eyes and sigh loudly. "That's an understatement!"

"That bad? Come on, what are you going as?"

"Little Red Riding Hood!"

"Are you kidding me? A sexy Little Red Riding Hood? I can't wait to see that…"

"What about you? What will you go as?"

"Well, now you've told me that, the Big Bad Wolf, obviously!"

"No! You're not serious?!"

"Dead serious. I'm going shopping tomorrow!"

Later, we are lying side by side in bed. He has satisfied my desires once again and I am snuggled in his arms, savoring the feeling of his fingertips softly stroking my back.

"Can I ask you something?"

"Yes, of course."

"Earlier, you said you weren't as liberated as Chloé…"

"Yes, I did…"

"Does that mean you've never played with a partner?"

"What do you mean 'played?'"

"In bed…"

I go deep purple, like I do whenever the subject of sex comes up. "Uh… No. Let's just say it's always been pretty tame."

"Would you like us to play together?"

"Do you mean now?"

"No, not now, you've worn me out! But on Halloween, for example."

"What exactly do you mean by 'play?' Role-play and dressing up?"

"Not exactly, no! Do you trust me?"

"Yes, I trust you, Matt."

He rolls over and props himself up over me on his elbows, scanning my eyes. "Thank you, my angel. I think we're going to have a perfect evening."

"You're not going to tell me more?"

"Do I detect a hint of concern in your voice?"

"Hmmm… Just curiosity."

"You'll see!"

◎ ◎ ◎

On Friday evening, the night before the big party, we agree to meet at ten the next morning to decorate the pub. Matt is looking more mischievous than ever, and keeps shooting me sneaky little glances.

I try to figure out what's going on, but he has completely clammed up. Then, in an attempt to beat him at his own game, I refuse to show him my costume, although I do ask if Chloé and I can come to his place the next evening so we can get ready together. That, he's cool with.

I call Chloé, who is not only happy to be able to check out Matt's crib, but also can't wait to help me get ready and do my makeup. She tells me she'll deal with Sam afterwards, and I say a silent prayer for him.

◎ ◎ ◎

On Saturday morning, we swing by the apartment to pick up the painted planks for the wall hanging, then we join the others at the pub. We get to work on making it the most fun place in town. With Matt's help, I unload the boards. This is the first time he's seen them.

The work Lucas and I did leaves him speechless, and the others are equally dumbfounded.

"This is genius, kids!" Terrence enthuses.

"Yep, the competition might as well pack up and go home right now, we've got a winner!" Chris exclaims.

I'm thrilled with our work and with everyone's reactions.

Matt installs the panorama with Lucas and Chris. That leaves Sam, and as he comes into view, I give him a few tasks. "Sam, the garlands need hanging, the pumpkins have to be put out and lit, and the tables need decorating."

"Sure, I'll do anything for you."

"SAM!" Matt interjects.

"I mean, I'll do everything for you…"

"SAM!"

"Uh, no. I'll do it all… Why does it keep coming out wrong?"

As I watch him trying to find a way of expressing himself that doesn't sound like innuendo, I see Matt grinding his teeth and shooting daggers at him.

Poor Sam…

Tommy checks the fridges carefully, ensuring we have everything we need for the cocktails, and decorates the bar with the little wobbly skeletons.

We finish decorating at around three, and decide to all go out for pizza.

It's about five when we get back to Matt's. That gives us an hour before Chloé arrives. As the minutes tick by, I become more and unnerved by his nonchalance. He's taunting me! I don't know what he's plotting yet. I've racked my brains, but I've got no idea. He gets his costume out and tells me he'll get ready downstairs. Then he jumps in the shower and leaves me to brood over my questions alone.

When he emerges, he gives me a long look. "You're too nervous."

"No. I…"

"Stop torturing yourself! Come here."

He pulls me to him and takes me tenderly in his arms. I breathe in his warm, fresh, woody scent. With his bare chest and damp hair, he is the embodiment of sensuality. Just being in his arms calms me down. He always has this soothing effect on me. He raises my chin with his thumb and places a kiss on my lips.

"Let's have coffee, and then I've got a present for you."

Now he's really piqued my curiosity! I can't resist trying to get this secret out of him, but he's playing his cards very close to his chest. He leads me into the kitchen, makes us two steaming cups of coffee and sits facing me, a conspiratorial look in his eyes. "Are you planning on tormenting me much longer, Matt?"

He looks at the clock, which is now showing 5:30 PM and smiles. "Only for another fifteen minutes!" he says.

By the time we have finished our coffee, the minute hand is on the nine. He stands up, takes my hand and leads me into his bedroom. Then he sits me on the bed, opens a drawer, and pulls out a package wrapped in purple metallic foil, tied with a silver ribbon. He comes and sits next to me.

"Open it," he says, handing it to me.

I take the gift, unwrap it carefully, and open the white box inside. My eyes widen.

"It's a remote-controlled vibrator." Matt explains, cool as a cucumber. "Stand up."

I get off the bed, and he undoes my jeans, slides them down my legs then pulls them off over my feet. He takes his gift, which is mounted on a sort of stretchy G-string, and gently puts it on over my lace shorty.

"I'd like you to wear it tonight. Under your panties. Do you trust me?"

"Yes."

"Then listen…"

He gets a remote control out of the box and keeps talking. "This little device controls your vibrator. The vibrator is your toy, the remote control is mine."

"What, at the pub? You mean you're going to use it while I'm working?"

"Exactly. And only the two of us will know why you're getting hot…"

His burning gaze seems to engulf me, making me flush. He wraps his arms tightly around me.

"I promise you a pleasurable evening," he murmurs in my ear. "Will you play with me?"

He nibbles my earlobe and, as if by magic, all my doubts disappear. "Yes, Matt."

The doorbell rings and he looks at me with lust in his eyes, then walks out of the bedroom.

"I'll get it. Don't forget to wear your gift, angel!"

25. Halloween

When Chloé arrives, Matt leaves us to go get ready, giving me a wink.

Overexcited about tonight, Chloé is bouncing around all over the place, squealing at the decor in Matt's apartment.

"Whoa! Classy! No wonder you've deserted our home!"

"I've not deserted it! I'm just spending time with Matt."

"I'm not mad at you, sweetie, I'm really glad to see you happy again."

She has no idea how right she is! Thanks to Matt, I'll soon have my PESA certification (Personal, Emotional and Sexual Awakening).

I slip into the bedroom and change while Chloé is in the bathroom. I get out the lingerie I bought a few days earlier: a sublime, white lace set. I put the vibrator in place, intrigued by this accessory, then slip on the sexy tanga panties. I can't believe the cut! It doesn't leave much to the imagination, and unlike regular tanga panties, these come higher at the waist, with a kind of belt.

The matching bra is delicately decorated, with fine, cord straps. The result is breathtaking.

I put on my costume, my boots, and the choker, then leave the bedroom. Catwoman is waiting for me, perched on the sofa. When she sees me, she gives me a double thumbs-up, going from happy to overjoyed in the blink of an eye. That's my Chloé!

"Come here, I'll do your makeup."

We take our time choosing: smoky black to show off my blue eyes, a rosy-pink powder for my cheeks, and peachy lip-gloss.

"There, you look stunning! Your stockings are all wrong, though. I brought you a better pair."

She pulls out some white stockings, held up by a delicate, white lace garter. "Put these on!"

I slip back into the bedroom and slide my legs into the silky mesh. They're divine!

When I go back into the living room, Chloé applauds enthusiastically. "Perfect! My work here is done!"

We check the time: 8:45. Time to head down to the pub.

"Hey, you didn't tell me about Sam. What's he coming as?"

"You'll find out soon enough! Believe me, he won't be forgetting his escapade the other day! I don't think he'll try that again!"

"Chloé, what have you done now?"

But she just winks and pushes me towards the door.

I put on my red hood, and we go downstairs.

Chloé's latex costume hugs her figure perfectly. Armed with her whip, she looks totally terrifying, but glorious! The door between Matt's and the pub is locked, so we go in through the main entrance. The boys, all sitting at the bar chatting, suddenly fall silent as they take in our outfits.

"Holy shit! Unbelievable!" exclaims Lucas. He strides over to me, takes my hand, and twirls me around on the spot.

I blush, mortified. The guys are still gawking lustfully when Matt arrives. I think the fatal blow has been dealt: mouth hanging open, eyes popping out, he literally devours me with his gaze. I am looking at the Big Bad Wolf, and he is lustful, hungry and horny.

"Fuck!"

In a flash, he is at my side, lifting me up to carry me into the kitchen as he devours my mouth.

"You have no idea how hot you look in that outfit! The Big Bad Wolf has a Big Bad Boner... Show me, turn around! Shit! How am I supposed to get through the evening?"

He takes a step back. "Thanks, Chloé!" he shouts into the next room.

We hear laughter, and he comes closer to me, frowning.

"Turn around."

I turn my back to him, not sure what he wants, and he pushes himself up against me, one arm around my waist, the other sliding up my skirt.

"Just checking."

When his fingers find the vibrator, he heaves a sigh of satisfaction.

It's not only his touch that's making me tremble. The excitement of the unknown, of what he has planned for me tonight, fuels my desire. My body reacts instinctively, and a surge of heat overwhelms me, rushing straight to my cheeks.

"Mmmm... It's going to be a reaaaallly long evening. Come on, let's go join the others."

When we return, the guys wolf whistle and congratulate me on my outfit. "It's Chloé you should be congratulating, not me..."

I look at them one by one, checking out their costumes. Chris is dressed as Don Juan, of course. Tommy is a vampire, Lucas a Greek warrior, and Sam... Sam isn't there. "Hey, where's Sam?"

The pub door suddenly swings open.

"Here he..." Tommy says.

Oh my God! Chloé has outdone herself! Sam's hair is cotton candy pink. He is wearing a snout and a pig suit...

The laughing fit that follows could win an award! They pile it on, really letting him have it.

Tommy turns to Chloé, gasping for breath. "You have to tell us how you made him agree to dye his hair pink!"

"I didn't agree to anything at all!" Sam interjects. "I'm a victim, you gang of degenerates! She told me to take a shower. And that... that... She put hair dye in the shampoo! Then she dressed me up in this monstrosity."

The laughter just gets louder, and the guys all start applauding Chloé. Matt seizes this moment of euphoria to drag me behind the bar, right into a dark corner, and flirt with me outrageously.

Grinding his groin against mine, with his arms gripping the counter on either side of my hips, he puts his lips to my ear. "Did you know that Charles Perrault's version of *Little Red Riding Hood* has been distorted many times?" he whispers in my ear.

"Oh?"

"One of the most famous renditions is Tex Avery's *Red*

Hot Riding Hood from 1943: the wolf is a sexual predator, the grandmother lives on the top floor of a skyscraper, and Red Riding Hood works as a vamp in a Hollywood nightclub: a precursor to Marilyn Monroe."

"And? What happens?"

"Red Riding Hood drives the wolf crazy. He tries to seduce her, but she shuts him down and then goes to hide out at Grandma's. The wolf goes after her, but he only finds the grandmother, who despite her age, is particularly fond of horny wolves. So, trapped in her penthouse, Wolfie ends up throwing himself off the top of the skyscraper to escape the sloppy wet kisses of the crimson-clad granny. Then the wolf sees Red Riding Hood again, and commits suicide right in front of her. Although Tex Avery's cartoon was initially censored, G.I.s were allowed to watch the uncut version, thanks to their cleverly indulgent higher-ups. But tonight, kitten, it's not the wolf who is going to see red. Red Riding Hood is the one who's going to go out of her mind..."

He grazes my neck with his teeth, smiles at me, and takes my hand, leading me back to the others. This evening has clearly gotten off on the wrong foot. It has barely begun, and I already want Matt so very badly!

The customers start arriving at around ten.

The tables start filling up with large parties of people, and the evening is crazy busy from the start.

Matt is on stage with the musicians, doing sound checks and setting up. I start taking orders, but I'm not used to serving customers in such an... enticing outfit.

I get to a table, my tray loaded with all different kinds of cocktails, when an intense vibration almost throws me off balance. The surprise and the sensation make me stumble, and I go as pink as a peony, but I manage, albeit just barely, to hang onto my tray and deflect disaster. When I look up towards the stage, Matt is crouched down, untangling cables, but his eyes are riveted on me. He chuckles, gives me a beguiling smile, and winks. It seems the fun has started, and it's going to be all I can do to stay focused and do my job calmly.

The music starts, creating a noisy, turbulent atmosphere, replete with monsters and witches. My wolf, a real beast on stage, is giving it his all, and the dance floor is suddenly packed with revelers thrashing about for all they are worth. I dare to hope that the intimate vibrations down under will be short-lived. Big mistake: just moments later, there is a second vibration, longer this time, sending shivers right down my inner thighs. Oh my God! I bite the insides of my cheeks, trying to contain the fire. The grip on my tray tightens. And Matt keeps right on singing, looking blissfully pleased with himself. Shit. How can he keep singing while he is torturing me like this? He relishes in the sight of me at the mercy of these delicious vibrations, his pupils dilated with pleasure.

He stops his onslaught for two seconds, only to intensify it. Shit! It's… it's… I clench my thighs together, trying to calm the sensation. It slowly recedes then stops. Matt runs his tongue over his lips hungrily, making me want him even more. I try to pull myself together and keep up with the infernal rhythm of the drink orders. Dammit, I'm burning up! At this rate, chances are slim that I'll survive the evening. The sensations are wonderfully thrilling, and fighting them takes all the strength I have.

As the night goes on, Matt's jarring attacks get more and more intense. I'm sweaty and breathless. Pleasure throbs throughout my entire body, ruled by his will. Controlling the game to perfection, he is clearly getting a kick out of seeing me twist and writhe. I nearly fall over about ten times, and it's sheer torture.

As my legs almost give way underneath me again, Lucas gabs me by the arm.

"Hey, Charlie, is everything okay?"

A new pulsation shakes my body and I can feel Matt's eyes on me, relishing the spectacle. When I answer Lucas, it comes out like a high-pitched whine.

"Yeees…Yes, I'm fine!"

He bursts out laughing, and asks kindly, "Are you sure? Because you're as red as a bet, and you look like you're feeling really flushed."

"Yes, I'm fine, promise. You're right, though, it really is hot in here."

"Take a break if you like!"

"No, it's okay. It's so busy, I'd rather carry on."

"Whatever you want, Charlie, but don't hesitate to take a break if you need one."

Hour after hour, my body is ravaged by Matt's relentless enthusiasm for his little game.

26. Free at Last

When Matt triggers the vibrator again, at an even more intense rhythm, I almost faint. I stumble to the bar, put down my tray, and grip the long brass pole around the edge as hard as I can. I try to contain this fire that is threatening to engulf me, swaying on my legs, when my diabolical, twisted wolf cranks the vibrations up to the max. The pleasure unfurls and my legs give way underneath me. I feel Matt's arms catch me and hold me up.

"Whoa, kitty… Do you feel weak?"

He pulls me to him and takes me into a dark corner. From here, we have a clear view of the crowd, but they can't see us. That is when I feel my gift pulsing wildly, and I lose it. Matt clamps a hand over my mouth and urges me to stop fighting, whispering words that are both sweet and seductive. When the orgasm comes, he has to hold me firmly against him so that I don't collapse.

"There, my angel… Gently now… Relax…"

He pushes me into the office, and locks the door behind him.

"Seeing you squirming all evening has been… more than I could have hoped for! Such self-control… But now, my angel, it's my turn to control you…"

My breath is still coming in short gasps, and I look at Matt with wide eyes. I am still subjugated by the orgasm he has just given me, and his words exhilarate me. The effect I have on him can be seen in his eyes. It's obvious how badly he wants me.

He puts one knee down on the ground and slides his hand up my skirt. When he discovers my panties, the look on his face tells me I chose well.

"Fuck! That's irresistible... God, you drive me crazy!"

He takes them off, and removes the vibrator, his touch unbearably soft. Then he gets up and plops me unceremoniously on the desk. His hand touches me intimately, and I hear him groan with pleasure.

"Mmmmmm... you're completely soaked!"

"I wonder why!"

"I love feeling you this ready for me... And right now, God, you're more than ready!"

"I want you so much I can't take any more, Matt. That gadget of yours is pure torture."

He smiles, a powerful, predatory expression on his lips, undoes his jeans and pulls out his cock, which is swollen with desire.

"Well, here's something else that might be too much for you to take. The Big Bad Wolf is hungry for you!"

He slips on a condom, spreads my legs, and drives himself into me with a powerful thrust of his hips. My muscles contract firmly around him as he pushes in. His smile is even wider now, even hungrier. He is savoring the heat of me around him. He pulls out almost entirely, before thrusting back in just as ferociously. He sinks into a steady, but savage and beastly rhythm, unleashing all of his energy, possessing me entirely. I am drunk on him, and he takes extravagant pleasure in filling me to the brim. His groans mingle with mine, and we drink each other in as I let go of three hours of built-up tension. Our orgasms explode together, in a thrilling whirlwind of pleasure.

When our finally catch our breath, he helps me up, and uses a fingertip to move aside a lock of hair that is stuck to my face.

"Phew, you unleashed the wolf, the stallion, and the whole zoo there..."

He bursts out laughing and rakes his fingers through his hair.

"Ha ha... Well, yes, they're difficult animals to tame, you know... a little on the wild side!"

Laughing, we readjust our outfits to make ourselves presentable, then we leave the office and head to the bar for a drink. Tommy serves us special Halloween cocktails, smiling to himself at a private joke. With a victorious laugh, Matt asks him,

"What, Tommy? What are you smirking at?"

"Oh, nothing, nothing. But I think it's Red Riding Hood who ends up inside the wolf, you know."

My already pink face turns scarlet, and I desperately want the earth to swallow me whole. Matt leans into me and gives me a reassuring kiss on the forehead. Tommy gives me a knowing wink at our obvious bliss.

"The Big Bad Wolf wanted to check out the goods."

"By eating Little Red Riding Hood aaaalll up?"

"It's because he has such biiiiig teeth!"

Matt gets up and tells us he's going back on stage. I start getting ready to go back to work as well.

"Can I borrow your sweetheart for a dance?" Chris asks Matt. "If she doesn't mind, of course."

"As long as you give her back afterwards... and keep your hands where I can see them!"

"You have my word as a gentleman!"

Chris offers me his hand with a little bow, and leads me over to the dance floor. With one hand on my waist and the other holding mine, he leads me in a slow dance. I can't help smiling at his courteous, gentlemanly attitude. "Wow, Chris, you're a great dancer! The ladies must love it."

"Isn't that one of Don Juan's distinctive qualities, my lovely demoiselle?"

"Sure, but I had no idea you had such hidden talents."

"There's more where this came from! One day, I'll show you how to salsa! It's much more... *caliente*!"

"You're awesome, Chris!"

Tommy comes over to us and announces that the next dance is his.

"Seriously, guys, I have to get back to work."

"Nah, tonight is Halloween! Everyone should enjoy it. Even us! Come on, Chris, hand her over and let me have a turn!"

In less than five seconds, I find myself in Tommy's arms. "This is ridiculous, I've got drinks to serve..."

"Well, I think you need to recover first!"

I go crimson again, which makes him double up laughing.

"Hey, stop blushing, Charlie! There's no harm in being good

to yourself! It's fine. You've joined a team made up almost entirely of men. We're no saints, and we all have moments of indulgence. Don't be embarrassed! Not with us... There's not a single one of us who would have been able to resist your little dress if we were in Matt's position. Let's just say you make a winning Little Red Riding Hood!"

"On the subject of winning, Spartacus, you're into contact sports, right?"

"Yep!"

"And do you fight a lot? How can you go into the ring, knowing it's going to hurt?"

"It's like Nietzsche said: 'He who fights too long against dragons becomes a dragon himself.'"

"But aren't you afraid when you face your opponents?"

"Not really, no. The first enemy you have to fight is inside yourself. It's often the only enemy. And no, I didn't come up with that. Christine Orban did!"

"What, the French literary critic? The novelist? You've heard of her?"

His face becomes roguish and enigmatic. "What? Boxers aren't allowed to like reading?" he says, spinning me around. "How prejudiced!"

The music stops, and we go back to the bar.

"Thanks for the dance, Charlie."

"My pleasure, Tommy!"

The last customers leave the pub at around 2:30 AM. We're all virtually dead on our feet, summoning the last of our strength to tidy up, before we head home for some well-earned rest. As we walk into Matt's apartment, I check my watch: 3 AM... No wonder I'm bushed! Aside from the fact that so many people came to the party, there's another reason for my fatigue. My whole body is still feeling the after-effects of my erotic experience. Anxiety suddenly floods through me.

"Shit, Matt, the vibrator..."

"What about it? Do you miss it already? Wow, you could compete in the Olympics..."

"No! We left it in the office!"

"Don't worry, I put it somewhere safe. No need to panic.

Your little toy is hidden. No one will find it!"

Relieved, I let out a long sigh. Matt smiles and walks over to hold me in his arms. "What would you say to some sleep, beautiful? I don't think you're in any shape for another round... Or am I wrong?"

"Oh Matt... Do you know how exhausting you were tonight?"

"And you didn't like it?"

"I never said that. I'd say it was a challenging but deliciously stimulating experience."

"Come on then. You've earned your rest."

As we slide under the thick duvet together, I immediately know what it is to savor paradise. Curled up in his arms and exceedingly exhausted, I am asleep almost before my head hits the pillow.

27. Disillusionment

I am woken from my sleep by a strange sensation. I sit up in bed and notice that Matt isn't beside me.

But what really disturbs me is the abnormally heavy silence in the apartment. A glance at the alarm clock tells me it is only just 10 in the morning. I leap to my feet and head into the living room. Still no sign of Matt. I can tell something is off. I go into the kitchen, but no... although there is a note for me, placed in full view on the table.

I had to leave urgently for work.
I didn't have the heart to wake you.
You looked like an angel.
I'll be away this week. I'll call you a.s.a.p.
Matt xox

What the hell is this? It's Sunday!

I snatch up my phone and try to call him, because I really need answers here, but it goes straight to voicemail. Fuming, I begin to pace around the apartment. Great! Just great! He's gone off without an explanation again, and of course, I can't reach him. I try to calm down and put things in perspective, searching for a viable excuse. But I can't find one. Dashing off urgently on a Sunday morning for work, when his job is downstairs in the pub, seems a bit fishy. I decide to go take a shower and get home as quickly as possible.

Once I'm washed and dressed, I pick up my bag. I am about to leave when a light blinking on the computer desk catches my attention. His laptop is on. I go over to switch it off, even though

I'm furious. I don't want him to lose his data, especially if it's work stuff. So I open the laptop and what should I see but his emails. The ground falls out from underneath my feet as I read the message on the screen.

Matt,

As we discussed on the phone earlier, here's your ticket for São Paolo. The flight leaves at 9:15. See you at the airport. This week with you is going to be great fun.

Selena

The screen blurs as my eyes fill with tears. A surge of rage floods my body. He… He… He's been playing me! I feel so humiliated. How could he do this to me? I trusted him! He did everything in his power to make me give myself to him unreservedly. For what? So he could pull this shit on me? Nausea takes over. I slam the screen shut and fly out of there, slinging the keys into his mailbox as I go.

By the time I get home, I am so horrified I can barely function. My legs manage to keep going, but my mind has deserted me. I push the apartment door open and head straight into my room, praying I won't bump into anyone. Then I crumble onto my bed and unleash my grief. My heart feels ready to tear itself to shreds. My body is racked with sobs. I curl into a tiny ball as my empty stomach lurches, projecting the taste of bile into my mouth.

I stay there for hours, listlessly curled up in a fetal ball, hiding under my duvet. I didn't see it coming. I never suspected a thing. I am a wreck. Exhausted by my tears, I fall asleep: the only way my mind can escape.

◎ ◎ ◎

A cold draft wakes me. Chloé is sitting on the edge of the bed. She has just lifted the covers and is staring at me with concerned eyes.

"What's going on, Charlie? I just got in and the door wasn't locked. That's not like you!"

"I… I must have forgotten."

"And I've been trying to call you for over two hours. Did you forget to charge your phone again?"

"Shit! My phone! I left it in Matt's kitchen!"

"Oh, well, that's not a problem. We'll go and get it."

My face clouds and my tears suddenly spill over again. I try to control them, but to no avail. The pain sears through me as I think back to that email. Chloé takes my hands, trying to offer me support without knowing why I'm such a pathetic mess.

"Hey, hey… Shh, honey. Calm down and tell me everything."

Between sniffs, I tell her about Matt's latest disappearance and about finding the email.

"Oh shit! I can't believe it! What a scumbag! I'm sorry, Charlie. Especially as I'm largely to blame: I encouraged you to let your guard down with him."

"I know you just wanted to help, Chloé. I'm not mad at you. I'm mad at him! At that fucking liar! And there's no chance of getting my phone back: I put the keys in his mailbox…"

"I'm sure he'll try and get in touch with you."

"And I never want to speak to him again."

"I understand. But sooner or later, you two are going to have to talk. He's your boss!"

The tears start flowing even harder, and Chloé takes me in her arms to soothe my shaking body.

She consoles me for almost an hour, pulling out all the stops to try and ease the pain that is plaguing me. "I… I love him."

"I know."

At around seven, I decide to take a few days off work. I don't want to see the guys at the pub, and going back there is just too painful. Everything at the Green Country reminds me of Matt. It's more than I can bear…

◎ ◎ ◎

The next two days are hell. I swing wildly between tears and nausea, drifting from room to room like a zombie. Chloé forces me to eat a little, but it's a lost cause. Nothing happens. Nothing. The pain doesn't subside, not even a little.

On Wednesday evening, Lucas drops by the apartment, since he can't get me on the phone.

"You're not answering your phone."

"I have no phone, Lucas."

"Well, that explains it. Hell, what's happened to you?"

"Nothing, Lucas, I just got involved with a total asshole!"

"Do you want to elaborate?"

"No."

Chloé comes in, brandishing a bottle of sweet white wine, which officially makes her my best friend for life! We uncork the bottle and, since it's his night off, Lucas stays and has a drink with us.

We avoid talking about Matt the prick, chatting instead about movies and songs, about anything really as long as nobody mentions him. On my eighth glass of wine, I feel numb. I'm starting to get really hammered, but God, I feel good! Finally, the pain has dulled.

"Charlie, you should slow down a bit. You haven't eaten anything."

"Chloé's right, you'll make yourself sick," Lucas agrees.

"Oh fffff… ffffuck off and leave me in beace… mease… peace! Can't I get drunnng without you bovvering me?"

I get up to go to the bathroom, but as soon as I am on my feet, the room starts spinning. Whoops! I lurch sideways. Lucas stops me from falling with an arm around my waist. "Oh shhpit… It's shhpinning. Haha! S'turning! Woooo…"

Chloé looks at Lucas, who almost splits his sides laughing.

"Uh, I think we've lost her…" he tells her.

Suddenly, a piercing sound assaults my eardrums. Shit, my head's going to explode…

Chloé picks up her phone, steps away for a minute, then comes back over to me, looking uneasy. "It's Matt. He wants to talk to you…"

I take the phone from her and start shrieking into it, "You know what, you can keep your spin… you shhpit… your spit… in your own filthy mouth… Asshole!!!"

"What's wrong?"

"Wha? Wasssrong??? I'm going out with a basdard shhhit who… who… had fuchked off to Brazil with the other airhead bimmm… bimbo. Y'no wha Matt? FUCK globetrotter mode. I am norrwilling to pay, to play Dora theshplor… theksch… fuckit… the explorer."

I'm hollering so hard I feel my stomach contract dangerously, and I clamp my hand over my mouth, letting the phone fall to the floor. Lucas realizes what is about to happen and rushes me into the bathroom, where I vomit lamentably into the toilet while he holds my hair out of my face. Once my stomach is empty, he carries me to my bed, tucks me in and kisses me on the brow.

"Bed time, Sue Ellen! Sleep well… you certainly need it, you little drunkard."

◎ ◎ ◎

At some point on Thursday morning, I emerge, obviously boasting a phenomenal hangover. I'm in a disastrous state: puffy eyes, fried brain, and my stomach is churning constantly. I just want some merciful soul to finish me off.

I mope around for most of the day, going from bed to sofa, then sofa to bed. All of my thoughts lead to the same destination: Matt.

At around six that evening, Chloé charges into the apartment.

"Charlie, Charlie! Where are you, dammit?"

She finds me, burrowed under my covers, holding Mister Rabbit Water in my arms.

"Matt's back! You have to go and see him."

"Surely you jest!"

"You have to talk to him. Really you do. You can't stay like this, you need answers."

"No!"

"Charlie! You need to get your phone back in any event. Come on, move!"

"No! Christ! Have you gone over to the dark side or what?"

"Charlie, he got home about an hour ago, and you need to go and see him."

"If he wants to see me so desperately, why hasn't he come here?"

"I don't know. But judging from his voice, he's not doing too well. He called me and asked me to pass on the message."

"What? On top of all the rest, he thinks he has the right to be angry?! Priceless! He's the one who can't keep it in his pants, and now His Majesty is making demands? Unbelievable!"

"I never said he was angry, Charlie, I said his tone was worrying. I'm telling you, he scared me. He sounded devastated. Lost and desperate."

Anxiety grips me. I can't help but shiver as I register what Chloé is telling me. Even in the worst of times, I know she chooses her words with care...

28. Revelations and an Angel

"He needs you, but that doesn't mean you have to go."

"I don't know if I have the courage."

"Courage means facing the truth inside you, accepting the obvious. You love him, don't you?"

"Yes, I love him. But…"

"So you do have the courage… you've admitted it. That was the hardest part, so no buts… Go and see him! You'll have plenty of time to think about it afterwards."

An hour and a half later, I am standing, petrified, in front of Matt's door. I'm so stressed out… I ring the bell and the door opens. I drag myself up the stairs and knock at the second door before I lose my nerve and turn back.

I hear him calling me to come in, so I turn the handle and walk into the corridor. He appears in the living room doorway. Tensely running a hand through his hair, he looks so… lost. Seeing him like this, I instantly start to worry. A thousand questions invade my brain, but I don't have time to think about them before I see a movement behind his leg.

A little boy, who looks about three years old, detaches himself from Matt's leg, trailing a comfort blanket on the floor behind him. His chestnut-brown eyes are clouded with tears, as if he is grieving greatly. I'm frozen on the spot. My mouth hangs open. His warm, olive skin suggests Latino origins, but the operative question here has nothing to do with his nationality. "Matt… I… Who is this?"

The little angel looks at me with big, gentle eyes, and makes a tentative movement towards me. Not quite sure how to act, I slowly crouch down, trying not to move too fast, then kneel on the ground. This seems to gain his trust, and before I know what's happening, he throws himself into my arms and starts crying again. I don't want to let him go, so I stand up and start rocking him gently.

"Help me," Matt says. "I'm stumped. I can't get him to calm down. Afterwards, I'll explain everything. But first, we need to get him squared away."

"Okay, Matt. Has he eaten?"

"No, not yet, we arrived about two hours ago, and he's been crying ever since. I don't even know what to give him."

Matt seems totally disoriented and powerless in the face of this child's tears.

"Do you have any mashed potatoes? Ham? Yogurt?"

"Yes, yes, hold on, I'll get them."

I keep rocking the little boy. He has wrapped one arm around my neck and is clinging to me like a terrified baby koala. I tell Matt to shred the ham. He prepares the food, since both my arms are full of child. Once it's ready, I sit down, getting the boy comfortable on my knee, and miraculously, he eats every forkful I give him. Matt observes us with great interest, the situation clearly beyond him. When the plate is empty, I try to put the boy down, but he categorically refuses to let go. I look at the clock. It's past eight-thirty. This kid really needs to get some rest. He's exhausted from all the crying. Children just can't cope when they are this tired. "He needs to sleep!"

"No kidding! But he doesn't seem to think so. I don't know what to do! I'm totally at a loss!"

"Do you have somewhere he can sleep?"

"Yes, there's a cot in my bedroom."

"We need to calm him down first. I've got an idea: get your guitar."

I settle down comfortably, with the child in my arms, and start rocking him very gently. Matt sits down next to us, with his guitar in hand. "Do you know any lullabies?"

"Not really, no…"

I think for a moment, then an idea flashes into my mind.

Initially, I thought of getting him to play a traditional lullaby, but since there aren't any of those in his repertoire, we'll have to be creative. "Do you know Sarah McLachlan? 'In the arms of an angel?'"

"Yes, I know it. I can play it, but I can't sing it. It's way out of my—"

"I'm not asking you to sing, Matt. Just play for me, will you?"

He looks at me strangely, stunned, and positions his guitar on his lap.

As he plays the first chords, I sing softly, all the while rocking the little boy in my arms. I croon in his ear, trying to give him the comfort and peace he needs to drift off.

Spend all your time waiting
For that second chance,
For a break that would make it okay.
There's always some reason
To feel not good enough
And it's hard at the end of the day.
I need some distraction,
Oh beautiful release.
Memories seep from my veins.
Let me be empty
Oh, and weightless, and maybe
I'll find some peace tonight.
In the arms of the angel,
Fly away from here
From this dark, cold hotel room,
And the endlessness that you fear.
You are pulled from the wreckage
Of your silent reverie.
You're in the arms of the angel.
May you find some comfort here.

Matt seems unable to take his eyes off me, as if he's seeing me for the first time, discovering my voice as it soothes this little angel. I close my eyes and continue my melodious song, filled with sadness and melancholy.

Gradually, I feel the little one's breathing become relaxed

against my chest, and I keep gently stroking his back. Matt's eyes burn into my skin, his gaze never leaving me. He makes no effort to hide his astonishment or his admiration. I am holding back the tears. Being this way with the man I love and this little boy ties my stomach in knots. I swallow back my sobs, and keep singing, attentive to every single breath coming out of his little mouth. When I finish the song, he is fast asleep in my arms.

"He's asleep. Your voice! It's… wonderful."

"Let's get him to bed."

We stand up as quietly as possible, and go to put the little darling in his bed, then head back into the living room.

Matt gestures for me to sit down on the sofa. "His name is Tao," he says, answering my question before I can ask it.

"But, who is this kid, Matt? Is he your son?"

"No, Tao's not my son, but I'm looking after him for a while. Let me explain. I'd better start from the beginning. God, it's a long story. There's so much to tell."

I'm not sure what to expect. I'm in a state of shock. My emotions are doing acrobatics, and it feels like my heart is skipping every other beat.

He sits next to me, rubbing his hands on his jeans, fidgety with stress.

"Okay, the first thing is, I don't give a damn about Selena, and you need to get that into your skull. She's nothing but a small insignificant part of the story, but I'll come back to that later. As I was saying, you'll only understand if I start at the beginning."

"Right, I'm listening."

"Good. When I was in the army, we'd marked out a sector that had been heavily planted with mines by arms traffickers. One morning, my unit and I were sent to inspect the site and make sure the warning signs were still in place. When we got there, there was a little boy right in the middle of the minefield. His kite had landed there, and he had gone to get it back."

My hand flies to my mouth, as I imagine the scene. "Oh my God! Matt…"

"We had to get him out of there right away, so I went in to help get him out of that hellhole… But the language barrier complicated things. He didn't understand what I was trying to say, and even when I held out my hand to him, he didn't move." He pauses, trying to control his halted breathing. He gets up and paces around the room, his eyes lost in the distance, veiled with pain. "I... I wanted to get a bit closer, but, but... he got spooked. His foot hit the trigger device. I tried to run towards him to stop him from removing his foot, but when I was about five or six yards away, he looked up and decided to walk towards me. I tried... but... the mine exploded, throwing me a few yards from his body. I couldn't save him."

I can feel the rage engulfing him as he speaks. His fists are clenched so hard I'm worried his knuckles will break. He sits back down, covering his face with his hands as if it might block out the horrendous memories.

"I left the army the same year and joined the humanitarian forces, undoubtedly to try and make up for it. To try and save children in a different way, to succeed where I had failed before. But out there, however hard we try, it's difficult to provide help. The medical facilities are outdated, and the kids often need more than we are able to give. Lots of kids end up mutilated because of those fucking mines. I quickly realized that on-site actions weren't enough." He fiddles with the edge of his sweater, trying to find the right words. "So I came back to France and I started an association called 'Among the Angels.' It focuses on providing surgery through skilled patronage. Millions of children around the world are suffering. They are victims of their birthplace, condemned because they can't access care. We organize volunteer hosting and treatment for children who wouldn't stand a chance in their own country, because the infrastructure just isn't there. Our services include diagnosis by on-site doctors, bringing the children to France, placing them in a host family, surgery and convalescence, and then returning them to their families. The children meet their host families at the airport. Their generosity allows us to keep the time that the children spend in expensive, specialized facilities to a minimum. They make it easier for the children by providing safe haven and support. Their kindness and companionship throughout the stay are critical. They live close to the partner hospitals and make themselves available for a period of eight weeks."

I look at him, unable to process it all. I'm trapped in an

emotional vise, and I feel nauseous. How could I ever have doubted him? But then again, how could I have doubted myself? So many things unsaid…

"Tao is one of these angels. He needs open-heart surgery in a week. I met him and his parents a year ago, on one of my trips. The reason I left on Sunday was to go get him. The formalities were taken care of, but his trip to France and his surgery were on hold. The host family dropped out at the last minute. That's why he's here. As for Selena, her father is one of the surgeons at the center. He brought her onto the team to try and knock some sense into her. She's a fickle, spoiled little brat. I forwarded her email to her father, so that he would know she didn't belong in the association. As soon as we landed, she was taken off the team."

"Matt, I… I'm sorry, I don't know what to say. Forgive me for doubting you, but all those trips, not knowing where you were… and… oohhhh shit! I shouldn't have gotten angry like that. You're the kindest person I've ever met. You…"

I kneel in front of him, clasping his hands in mine, unable to stop the tears. But he tenses up like a bowstring, his teeth clenched, and pushes my hands away. "No, don't say that. I'm a selfish monster."

"What? How? What are you talking about? You can't say that! You're anything but selfish, Matt. You…"

"Charlotte! I AM SELFISH! I let you get attached to me, I even encouraged you to do it, because I couldn't bear the thought of losing you. I was only thinking of myself. And you… Seeing you with Tao just now, I realize I have to let you go. I can't give you what you want. You deserve so much better than me."

"No, Matt, stop! I don't want to hear you say that. You can't say that."

"Dammit, Charlotte, listen to what I'm telling you! I can never make your life complete! When the mine exploded, I was injured… I can't have children. I can't make you a mother. And you're so full of maternal love and kindness. Just look at Tao, how he responded to you… I… I'm sorry."

I feel like he's just slapped me in the face! All the blood drains away from my cheeks, leaving me pale. "Oh! Matt… I'm the one who's sorry—I should have tried to find the strength to talk to you about it earlier. There are nightmares that just keep haunting you, even after your eyes have opened. I... I can't have children either, Matt..."

This time, the levee breaks and my tears come gushing out. My sobs are devastating and uncontrollable.

"What? But... why?"

He nervously runs his hands through his hair and comes to sit on the floor with me, taking me in his arms and rocking me. "After what happened to me, I found out I was pregnant, but the trauma of it all triggered internal bleeding. The doctors had to do a full hysterectomy, depriving me of the chance to become a mother forever. I couldn't find the strength to tell you, because to me, that meant losing you. I didn't have the right to drag you into my misfortune. That was why I wouldn't tell you that I love you, Matt."

"You... You love me?"

"More than you'll ever know, Matt!"

"Why didn't we tell each other all this earlier?"

"Because pain can seal your lips, and instill fear of the future... I love you so much, Matt!"

Epilogue

Two months later, we are all together in the pub. It's time to celebrate! Chris and Tommy are laughing like kids, bobbing around to the music.

Chloé and Sam are here, but haven't made up. They alternate between dark glares and ignoring one another. Since I've been so busy with things recently, Chloé just told me that she would explain everything in good time.

I hope so!

Terrence, perched on his stool, is the same as always: reserved, but a good guy. The gentle giant supervising our gang. I go over to him to ask a question that's been burning my lips for a while now. "Terrence, Matt mentioned that everyone voted on whether or not to have a girl on the team. I was just wondering why you agreed to take me on?"

He looks up at me, with a strange smile on his face. "For them, Charlie," he answers, pointing to the team. "And for him," he adds, nodding towards Matt. "When you came here for the first time, you were like a terrified little kitten, but you had the determination and courage of a lioness. Most of the girls who applied here did so because of the reputation of this place, or in the hopes of getting a guy into bed. You were sincere. And look! Look where you and Matt are now…"

I turn away for a second to observe Tao. He is sitting on the bar, a big grin on his face, while Matt and Lucas teach him how to use a cocktail shaker. So much has happened! The week following Matt's revelation was emotionally intense. We were doing all we could to make Tao comfortable and get him to trust us: taking him to city parks, trips to the zoo, buying him candy... everything in our power to make his time here easier. We formed special bond.

We had never prayed so much in our lives as we did on the day of the operation. Praying for everything to go well. Praying for this little angel to get the very best care, so that he wouldn't have to tame his childish enthusiasm were his little heart to stop. Matt was as nervous as I was, but he tried to reassure me as best as he could and explain every stage of the process. But then we got some awful news. While little Tao was fighting bravely on the operating table, there had been a coup in Brazil, and his parents had been found dead. The news left us devastated. What would happen to the little angel now? We had become so attached to him. His heart might have been in good hands with the surgeons, but ours were breaking, knowing how hard things would be for him.

The operation was a great success. Tao would be able to lead a normal life, but he had lost the only family he had left.

We found ourselves in a situation that the organization had never had to face before, and everyone kept saying the most unbearable things.

"It won't be easy to place him."

"Social services have been notified."

"We can put him in a home..."

These statements disgusted me... They disgusted *us*. This fragile little angel had already been through too many horrors, and now, they were talking about placing him, like a lost object on a shelf.

The whole team rallied around us through this difficult time and supported us tirelessly. As for Matt, he fought a fierce and relentless battle against the system.

What I learned that day turned our lives around. It left us confident about our determination to find a solution worthy of our undying love.

"Listen to me carefully, kitten. I want to apply to adopt Tao. Since I've hosted him in France, I'll get priority. All I have to do is sign. I... I'd like to know if you would agree to join me in this adventure and spend the rest of your life with me... make me a father, a husband, a lover, make me whatever you like, as long as you say yes..."

My legs buckled beneath me. That was the last thing I expected. But it was the first thing I wanted. Yes, spend the rest of my days loving him, loving both of them... I threw my arms around his neck, passionately kissing this unique, proud, and sensitive man, this irresistibly alluring, sensual, strong, and kind man. My man! The man I said yes to...

Today, we're celebrating our official adoption of Tao. As I look at the two of them, I realize how happy I am. I have all I could ever wish for: my man... my child... and our friends.

Acknowledgments

I would especially like to thank all the people who are there for me in my day-to-day life, for their support, and for understanding that I need to cut myself off from the world from time to time.

Thank you to the man in my life, who has supported me unconditionally and completely on my madcap mission to write this story. My very own super-hero has never failed to help me work through my fears, my uncertainties, my psychological absences, the unconventional mealtimes… basically, everything that happens to you when you go into your little writing bubble.

A huge thank you to my crazy friends…

Above all, my three psychos!

Marie, who gave me the idea in the first place: part unicorn, part ferret, all love. Meeting you changed my life and was the start of a deep, unwavering friendship. I'm proud to know you.

Claude, I am so lucky to have met you. We have shared our respective lunacies with each other, as well as lots of laughs, our passion for literature, and our weakness for bearded men. "Beardland," here we come…

Sissie, you have always been there for me… We have a wonderful friendship, which began with our evening chats and has been going strong ever since. Your writing has captivated me and your friendship has touched me deeply.

Also, Audrey, Florianne, Caroline… You guys have pushed me, encouraged me, inspired me. You have made me laugh and you have made me cry. Your presence during this adventure kept me going to the end!

Thank you! You rock, girls!

Thank you also to the bloggers, who do such an excellent job of their colossal task: promoting authors and their works. Thank you for putting such passion into your blogs, and for your amazing devotion to the literary world.

And above all, a huge thanks to *Les Éditions addictives*, for believing in me and giving me the chance to tell you this tale. You're the best!

**Other novels from
WARM PUBLISHING**

My Hipster Santa
by *Mag Maury*

In Liverpool, the barbershop Hipster Maniac is an institution. Run by three bearded, tattooed friends, it is the place to listen to great rock, get a trim, and have a drink.

But for Line, it also spelled trouble. For starters, when she first got to the neighborhood, she rear-ended Jordan's car, who turned out to be one of the three barbers. Then she discovered that they were neighbors in business and residence! So no way can she escape this muscle-flaunting, smoldering man who is covered in tattoos and... completely insufferable!

He draws her near only to push her away. He toys with her shamelessly. But worst of all he hates Christmas whereas that is Line's very favorite time of year!

Beneath a backdrop of festive fairy lights, intoxicatingly passionate kisses, and blistering banter... It's on!

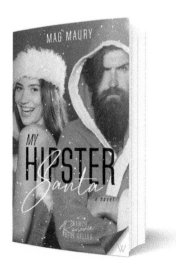

My Stepbrother: A Sexual Revelation
by *Sophie S. Pierucci*

Cassie is a highly intelligent young woman... Too much so for her own good! And she is as daunting as she is intriguing. Carl, the son of his father's second wife, would hardly say otherwise!

Carl is the exact opposite of his steady father. He is a player and a slayer. Afraid of nothing and no one. Except for Cassie when she asks him to introduce her to the pleasures of the flesh.

And when the situation gets out of control, it is too late to turn back, and the two lovers find themselves ensnared in forbidden passion. Forbidden by everyone: society, their parents, their friends.

But how to resist the desire that consumes them?

The Amicable Pact
by *Ana K. Anderson*

She is about to get married. But not to him.

Quinn MacFayden, an accomplished expat businessman in New York, is set to return to Scotland in extremis to protect the precious family legacy. His 91-year-old grandfather is about to marry a perfect stranger sixty-six years his junior... And that is out of the question! Quinn swears it. Over his dead body will Dawn Fleming ever be part of the family!

But Dawn is not a future bride like the others. She is nowhere near the gold digger he imagined and, above all, she knows just how to stand up to him. And so a game of cat and mouse begins between them. A war with no holds barred and where surrender has never been so tempting...

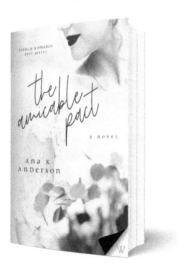

About the Author

 Budding French author, Mag Maury, was showcased at the Paris Book fair in 2018 and is a rapidly rising star on the French literary scene.

Before becoming an author, she trained as a medical secretary then and decided to change careers and went into infographics. She actually started writing on a dare while she was bedridden after a serious operation. Once her first novel was complete, a friend encouraged her to submit it to a publisher and she did. Her career went uphill very quickly thereafter owing to her very charismatic novels that are as energetic as they are entertaining.

Mag is a self-professed compulsive reader who likes a wide variety of literature especially dark romanticism, urban fantasy and new adult fiction. She also likes country music, long walks and fine cooking. In addition, her creative spirit has led her into the world of visual art where her work has won awards.

Originally from Nîmes, she currently lives in a quaint river-adjacent cottage at the foot of the Cevennes with her significant other—an accomplished athlete who is her own personal superhero—and her Yorkie, Fanou. In the summer you can often find her down by the river and in the winter, at home, in front of a roaring fire.

Lightning Source UK Ltd.
Milton Keynes UK
UKHW010741261021
392864UK00002B/319